ANCESTRAL WHISPERS

BRIAR O'PATRICK

Copyright ©2025 Line By Lion Publications
 www.pixelandpen.studio
ISBN:979-8-9988123-0-9

Edited by Susan Prather
Cover Design by Thomas Lamkin Jr.

For more information, email www.linebylionpublications.com

Dedicated to my former romantic partners. You gave me many reasons to daydream about the perfect partner. So I wrote about him. Take notes.

PROLOGUE

Morrigan ran through the Scottish countryside. She realized if she didn't shift shape, she would die. The wolf wasn't fast enough. These men were on horses, and they were catching up to her quickly. She had never shifted by her need alone; rather, it was always to help others. She realized, in that instance, she was the one who needed help. She thought of something that would make it more difficult to be captured, or killed, she wasn't sure what exactly they wanted. Her mind raced, and then she knew what she must do. Before the eyes of the clan of men after her, she began to transform.

Her fur became feathers. She shrank substantially. Her front legs transformed into wings, and she flapped them as fast as she could. An eagle began to rise from the ground. She had a better chance. At least, that's what she thought until she saw one of the men raise a bow. He loosed an arrow and it pierced her right wing. She thought of another animal and transformed so she could make a smoother landing. Before their eyes, she changed into a shiny black panther, but she was taken aback. She couldn't run. Her right leg was a mangled mess from the arrow. She knew she couldn't get away. She grabbed the amulet around her neck and placed her life in the hands of the great creator. He had named her the lady eternal. She had been that for more than 100 years.

As she lay on the ground with the men surrounding her, she slowly transformed into a beautiful woman. A man stood behind her laughing maniacally.

"We dinnae waant witches or whitevur yer near us or oor families. Go back tae whaur ye cam fae!"

He picked her up by her red hair and slit her throat. The last thing she saw was her body lying on the ground as her spirit wisped away. When she saw her little house, she made her way inside. She floated next to her husband as he held her new son. Angus was such a blessing, and she knew what she must do. She watched as her magic entered her son. The Lady Eternal would always be around in some respect. One day, she would come back to her full power again. When her line next had a daughter strong enough to fight and help her community, she would be back.

CHAPTER ONE

I t's not that Mellie wasn't seen. Just that she didn't particularly want to be. She had set her life up that way. Sure, she had her family, and a couple close friends but she wouldn't consider herself outgoing and had no desire to be. She grew up on a farm in rural Ohio. It was only a 35 minute drive from Cleveland and subsequently her office. At the age of five it was only the ladies 10 out of 12 months a year. When her fifth birthday rolled around her dad and grandpa sat her down and explained to her that her dad would now be traveling with her grandpa for work. That was her dads thirtieth birthday. They would return every July and August. Sometimes having to work the weekends but there to make the memories. She celebrated those two months every year. More than she celebrated her birthday. Her birthday was July fifth, so always the first thing they celebrated. They'd do all their traveling and even celebrated holidays that they missed the rest of the year. It was incredible because it was the time of the year that Mellie was out of school, so she did everything with the two most important men in her life.

Her two best friends couldn't have been more different than each other, but they were both amazing and luckily loved each other as well as Mellie. Blair was a couple years older than Mellie. They had been best friends since preschool. Blair had blossomed into everything that anyone on the outside looking in would have wanted. Petite, tan, blonde hair and blue eyes that closely resembled the ocean. She was kind and generous. Not to mention extremely outgoing and a bit of a partier. She also worked at the magazine. She wrote every article in the fashion and beauty section for the last ten years. She had been offered bigger gigs with more money in bigger cities but had always turned them down. Cleveland was her city, and she didn't want to leave it or Mellie. As they grew up, they didn't stop being friends they had just grown apart. They had adopted the new role as work friends. Dinners near their birthdays and the occasional drink after work. Shawn was her lifelong best friend. He had lived next to Mellie for their whole lives. They did everything together for as long as both of them could remember. They helped each other on their farms. They went to dinner occasionally and they even celebrated birthdays like they were part of the family. As they had grown though he changed. He was a big man. At nearly 7 feet tall and close to 300 lbs. of muscle he was something that dreams were made of. Nellie of course kept her mouth shut on that subject. She knew he'd never find her attractive in the romantic way she wished he would.

Mellie had her dream job. Just so happens her dream job was mostly remote, so she didn't see anyone in the office much. She was the editor of the most popular magazine in the country and had worked her tail off to make that happen.

Mellie herself wasn't shy, but she didn't put herself out there like the people in her life would have wanted. She was tall for a woman at 5'9". Pale freckled skin with the most mysterious blue/gold eyes. They were her favorite feature about herself. She had won the eye genetic lottery thanks to her father and grandpa. She was a big girl. Not fat given her height but thicccck with 4 c's. It was in all the right places, but her size made her self-conscious, especially around Blair. Her hair was like a blazing fire. Almost to her waist.

She had formed a wonderful love of the outdoors which meant most of her was rock solid. She promptly covered that up with baggy clothes that made her look ten years older but she liked it that way. Her life was complete as far as she was concerned.

Until the morning of her 30th birthday that is.

CHAPTER TWO

Mellie rolled over grumbling and hit snooze on her phone alarm. It was her birthday after all, and she had given herself the extra time to rest. She didn't have big plans for that day outside of work. It was a Friday which happened to be her catch up day at work. Ten minutes later she slowly sat up, placed her amulet around her neck, and wished herself a happy birthday. Mellie's grandfather had given it to her for her birthday the year before. Her father and grandpa had just gotten back from their tenth month away. This year they had been building some new apartments in the ever-developing Kentucky countryside. Later that day she'd be headed home to celebrate with her family and her childhood best friend Shawn.

She sat on the edge of her bed and ran through her to-do list for the day.

* one more article to edit and send to Fiona, her boss, at Infinity Magazine
* meet with Blair for lunch before heading to the family farm.
* dinner with the family and planning their yearly camping/hiking trip.

When she finally had her bearings, she made her way to the bathroom. After taking a shower and drying her body she started her daily skin care routine. As she looked up, she let out a bloodcurdling scream!

Assuming she caught too quickly of a glance to actually see herself she slowly looked into the mirror again. "WHAT THE ACTUAL FUCK?!!" She was clearly looking at herself, but it wasn't 'herself'.

It's not like it wasn't her. It just wasn't the 'her' she'd looked at every day for the past thirty years. Her eyes were still blue/golden but more on the golden side. She was still tall but for some reason looked bigger. She was always strong, but she felt more powerful! No, she hadn't tried the theory out yet, but she just knew. Her hair was still the color of fire. Her freckles were there. It was her but just "better"? Maybe enhanced?

Who was this woman and where had she come from? She didn't know what to do.

Well, she did know what to do first. She had a unibrow!!! That would not be staying. She grabbed her facial razor.

Once completed, she ran through the day's itinerary again… She absolutely HAD to edit and turn in next week's article. "The ten ways to enjoy your life" article was easy enough seeing as her boss had written it. She loved her boss, but this article was not her speed. Too much on how love was the true definition of happiness. It wouldn't have bothered her if it meant all sides of love, but knowing Erica it was all about the romantic type of love. Mellie was very certain that love meant many different things and romantic love wasn't that important in the grand scheme of things.

About two hours later she pressed send on the article and could now focus on the main issue in her current life. What had happened in the span of eight hours of fitful sleep? She called Blair to confirm their lunch.

"What's up birthday bitch?!" Her best friend screamed over the phone.

"I KNOW IT'S HER BIRTHDAY, but you're at work. Keep it PG please!" Mellie heard Erica yell from Blair's side of the phone.

"Hey, lovely lady! Thanks! Still on for lunch?"

"Of course Mel! Wouldn't miss it for anything!"

"Alright! See you in a half an hour. Oh, by the way I don't look the same as I did yesterday." She hung up the phone.

"Ummmmm what do you mean?!…. HELLO!!!! Mel where are you?! I'm so confused. Damn it!!!! She hung up…."

CHAPTER THREE

Mellie hadn't a clue what to wear. Her body had changed so drastically nothing looked the same. Her belly, which could have been considered a small apron belly before, was completely flat. Her pectoral muscles had lifted her breasts so they were no longer even remotely sagging. Her ass which had always been nice was even more so. The clothes that used to bring her comfort and hideability now screamed "LOOK AT ME!" It was her birthday, she supposed she could deal with a little look at me. Mellie grabbed a black skirt that was just above the knee and now hugged every curve. She went with a burgundy crop top tee that now gave her cleavage new meaning. To keep it simple she put on her famous "Jesus sandals ", and her black crossbody bag.

Before she walked out the door she gave her mom a ring. She knew she'd have to leave a voicemail as it was midday during summer harvest, but she needed her mom to know big things had occurred.

'"Hey Mom! I'm going to lunch with Blair and then I'll be headed your way. We have A LOT to talk about."

She walked out the door and jumped in her car. It was a nice 2024 VW Gulf. It was a quick five minute drive. Mellie could have walked there but thought leaving the restaurant and heading straight to the farm was the best option. She pulled into the parking lot and saw Blair waiting in her car. Mellie started to get nervous, and she debated turning around. She wasn't quite sure she was ready, but as usual her friend read her mind.

"If you turn around, I'll follow you! Get your ass out of that car!" Was the text she received that made her pull into a spot. As she stepped out of her car she saw Blair's jaw drop.

"Who the hell are you and what did you do with my bestie?!"

"I don't know! See I told you! I woke up like this and I'm freaking out!! I was debating going to the office today, but decided against it because I couldn't handle everyone seeing me like this!"

"You look incredible girl! Let's go eat. We obviously have a lot to talk about." Blair declared.

After ordering drinks Mellie told Blair all about her morning and they brainstormed a million reasons this could have happened. They threw around the idea of "late puberty", "early menopause", "a new workout routine".... None of which were plausible. Mellie tried not to pay attention to all the side eyed glances she was receiving. She had never been the woman who had eyes on her and she liked it that way. Blair could see that Mellie was getting a little anxious.

"Hey, don't worry about it. I'm telling you now they're all good looks.

They can't take their eyes off the new you. I quite admire the new look too!" Mellie could feel her face growing warm. She wasn't sure how she felt about this new her, but the idea of eyes admiring her wasn't awful she supposed. The knowledge that she was attractive to her best friend, while flattering, was a bit weird.

After their drinks arrived, they ordered their meal. Blair ordered her normal Caesar salad and cheesy potato soup. Mellie on the other hand ordered a rare steak, a jacket potato and green beans. Her normal baked chicken and rice didn't sound even remotely appealing.

"So, Blair, anything interesting happen with you lately?"

"Now that you mention it… Not anything as crazy as your total transformation. However, I do think I may have met someone. Potentially special, but not sure quite yet. They are brilliant, and athletic. The most fun I've had outside of our adventures, maybe in my lifetime."

"That makes my heart so happy! You deserve someone who gives as much as you do."

When their lunch arrived, Mellie was so ravenous she barely spoke. She couldn't remember a time in her life when she had been so hungry. She would have to tell her dad and grandpa that she had tripped into another one of their traits. They always ate like they hadn't eaten in months. Mellie had joked with them about it for years. She had a sneaking suspicion they would get to give her all the payback in the world in the coming two months.

After finishing their lunch, they parted ways with a hug and promised to get drinks sometime in the next week. Mellie had also, in a moment of weakness, agreed to let Blair take her shopping as a birthday present. Mellie realized she needed new clothes for this new body and no one in her life knew fashion as well as Blair, but it simultaneously made her excited and extremely nervous.

They got in their cars and drove their separate directions. Blair, back to her office as Mellie headed out of town to go to the family farm. As she drove in the direction of her family she couldn't help but know that her life forever about to change.

CHAPTER FOUR

Farm life had been the only life Aileen and Amelia had ever known. They ran the family farm like a machine even though the men in their life weren't around very often they got everything they needed to do and more done. Today was like every other day, aside from the fact that earlier that morning their husbands had returned from their ten month job contract. Or at least that's the story they had gone with for the past twenty five years. Amelia's only child, a son named Callum and her husband Angus worked very hard most of the year and spent their two "free" months on the farm making memories and taking over most of the farm work from the ladies. It was nice to have the hottest months of the year not be so stressful. They had just ~~got~~ showered and changed when they heard what had to be Mellie's car pulling down the long drive. They knew they had about an hour until she walked through the door. Mellie, no matter how long she'd been away, whether a day or a month, always had to stop and love on all 20 of their horses. She usually stopped in their small personal garden to harvest what she could to take a little more weight off the rest of the family.

However, to their surprise and shock five minutes later she came barging through the door yelling, "Mom, Grandma!!!! What the hell happened to me!!! I fell asleep looking and feeling like every other day in my life and woke up like this! Please tell me someone knows something, anything!"

Amelia and Aileen came running into the kitchen and with looks of shock stopped in their tracks. They looked at her over and over while glancing back and forth for what seemed like forever.

Aileen grabbed her cell and rang Angus. "You and Callum need to get up to the house quickly. Mellie just got here, and you have to see something!"

"Is she ok?!" Exclaimed Callum in the background.

"She seems ok but different. 'Changed' somehow if you know what I mean. The same woman just stronger, her eyes are more golden. I don't fully understand, but I may have an idea."

Ten minutes later they were standing in front of Mellie with wide eyes and open mouths. It was one of the strangest moments of her life. Not quite as crazy as what had happened when she woke up that morning, but crazy just the same. Little did she know she wouldn't be seeing the end of strange, anytime soon.

Callum and Angus stared at her, giving each other sideways glances. They thought they knew what was happening, but they didn't think it was possible. At least in every family journal there had never been a female with their gift. They thought it would skip her completely and if and when she had a son their gift would be passed down to him. Never in a million years did they think they'd have to have this conversation with Mellie. If they had known they would have begun the training and explaining part of this years and years ago. Not now, just two months from her first big, life altering ten month change…

Mellie could see the fear, shock and disbelief in the four sets of eyes that were staring straight back at her.

"So, you all know what's happening to me?! Please explain why I woke up jacked and with a damn UNIBROW!!"

"Honey," said Amelia in her sweet, comforting voice. "Let's sit down and enjoy each other's company for a bit. We will talk about everything after dinner. You also may need to take up Fiona's offer to go fully remote for work."

"Why does this feel like the beginning of a horror movie?"

"Mellie… It's not a horror movie. Just the beginning of a new adventure. Come eat, Mellie. We'll explain everything."

"Ok Mom. Not to be harsh but your constant optimism is incredibly annoying right now." Mellie said with a great big sigh. Mellie hadn't even noticed in all the chaos that they had decorated the entire house. There were red and black table clothes, streamers and balloons everywhere. It wasn't childlike. Everything looked very regal and sophisticated. There was an enormous cake on the table and wrapped packages. She had always loved her birthday more than any other day of the year. Not for the reason that kids loved their birthdays, but because it was the start of the two months a year she got to spend with her whole family. She had a feeling that this year would be very, very different.

She sat down at the table and her family started bringing out the meal. They would come out of the kitchen smiling but she could hear them talking amongst themselves every time they went back in the other room. When all the food was sat on the table Angus walked into his office and came back with a large pile of books.

"First things first" he said as he dropped the books on the floor between him and Amelia, "We eat and celebrate then we get down to business."

Mellie looked at the large spread of food on the table. Ribeye steaks, ribs from the slow cooker, rotisserie chicken, jacket potatoes, corn, two different kinds of salad and all the bread you could imagine. The family didn't eat this way all the time. Only when the guys were home. She had never seen anyone eat like them. That is, until she had eaten that way just today at lunch with Blair. She decided not to pick on them about it, but instead just demonstrate. Mellie grabbed an inch-thick steak, an entire rack of ribs, two chicken legs, and roughly two portion sizes of every side on the table. Let's not forget the bread slathered with butter. By the time the strangely quiet dinner was over she herself had polished off every bit of food and close to half a loaf of fresh bread.

They decided to wait on the cake and found their cozy seats in the living room.

CHAPTER FIVE

Angus started the conversation very apologetically. "Sweet girl. First, we want to apologize for not preparing you for this sooner. Had we known a female could carry this gift we would have started training roughly 25 years ago. You see, our family comes from an ancient line of gifted people. Before we talk about it in detail, I want you to take a look at these books I've brought out. I know you've heard the folklore about the Scottish Wulver. They aren't just a story dear. Our family carries the line, and these books will tell you all you need to know initially."

"Ok Grandpa. I'll look through them. When I'm done, we'll have to sit down and actually talk." She stood up and grabbed the giant stack of books.

"Sweety," Callum called, "I know this is strange and new. Trust me it was to me as well, but we'll get through it together. While you're doing your research Grandpa and I will also be looking into it. As far as we can tell there's never been a female of our kind. Hopefully we can find reference somewhere to help us navigate this path better. I love you sweety."

"I love you too and I'm so glad you're home when I'm going through this." She walked up the stairs and into her childhood bedroom. It was still painted in her favorite girlhood colors, purple and pink. Her mother had, however, gotten a bigger bed and added some more adult decor. She plopped the books on her desk and flipped her laptop open. She logged into her work email. The article she had sent in earlier that day had been approved for print.

A couple of weeks before Mellie's birthday, while she was in the office, Fiona had come to her with the option to be fully remote. It wasn't because they didn't want her there. It was because Mellie seemed to get so overwhelmed with all the people running around. It was something she had been considering. With all the things that had changed in just a day, Mellie decided to take the offer. She hit compose and started an email to her boss.

Fiona,
After much thought and deliberation, I will be accepting your fully remote position. I would still like to be a part of the meetings so expect me to be there virtually.
I will have the rest of this week's articles to you by the end of business day tomorrow.
Thank you for this opportunity.
Sincerely,
Mellie Murray

She sat down on her bed and picked up the first book in the extensive pile they'd handed her. "The Murray Family Line", Ok, she thought the perfect place to start. She opened the book to a huge family tree. It wasn't like any she had seen before. She supposed it was a normal one however, as the only ones she'd ever seen were Ancestry.com trees her friends had posted on social media. She hadn't yet completed one because, to be honest up until this very day it hadn't really interested her. She knew where she was from, her nationality, and all the family she thought she had ever needed.

The part of the tree that struck her as strange was how very male dominated her lineage was. Most of the descendants were men. I mean sure they sprinkled a few females in the mix but all in all testosterone reigned supreme. The other thing that she noticed was the fact that one male, specifically the oldest in the generation, had a small mark next to their name. It was a symbol she'd never seen before. It looked like a family crest but not the Murray family crest. It looked like a large set of eyes peeking out of a cave. It then had the regular things every crest she'd ever seen had. A scroll with Murray written in and olive branches surrounding it. She knew the olive tree meant virtue and strength. Everything else she'd have to ask about.

As she glanced through the rest of the book she came to the realization that every man with the strange crest kind of disappeared in a sense the year of their thirtieth birthday. This made sense as it was exactly how her father and grandpa lived their lives. She decided to put that book down and grab the next.

This book was entitled, "How it all Began, The Murray Line", This one she hoped was a little more helpful than the last. While interesting, the family tree book hadn't given her much insight. In fact, it had left her with more questions than answers. As she opened the book to the first chapter it dawned on her that this was going to take a long time. She wished there was an audio version so she could do something else while listening. Crochet, Clean, or even take notes. She would have preferred to enjoy her regular family custom of watching a movie with her parents while her grandparents sat on the porch enjoying the cool night air. However, here she lay reading all about something she had no clue would even help her. She decided to go grab some tea and a snack from the kitchen.

As she hit the bottom of the landing, she saw her mom and grandma pacing back and forth while her father and grandpa sat at the table in deep conversation.

They saw her and became still.

"Don't worry I've just finished the family tree. I've written down some questions but that can wait as I've just picked up the second book. It doesn't look like it's been read through though. Is it important enough to waste time on?" she asked.

"Yes sweety. I would say it's probably the most important. It hasn't been read because the men in this family have had their entire lives to know what and who they are. Not to mention the job entrusted to them. Please read that one carefully and let us know what you find." Her dad said.

"Alright Dad. Let me grab some nourishment. Maybe coffee is a better idea than the tea I was thinking about."

"Yeah, you're probably right about that. Sorry we didn't get a chance to really enjoy your big day. We'll make it up to you!" Her grandpa said while looking like he knew he had broken her heart. She grabbed her food and caffeine, walked up the stairs and got to reading.

CHAPTER SIX

She knew she had been right about the book never being touched. When she opened the book, she cracked the binding. She knew she was in for the ride of a lifetime. She didn't understand why no one had read it before. She decided to ask her dad later.

As she read through the first few pages her eyes grew larger and larger. What she read scared her more than anything she'd ever read in her life. Which was crazy, as she edited more articles about the paranormal than anything else. It most likely scared her more because it was her life. Her actual life, and fuck if that wasn't terrifying. The coffee, or maybe the interest in what her life was becoming made her finish in record time. She jotted down anything of importance, grabbed the book and ran down the stairs. She must have taken longer than she thought because the house was dark and quiet. She realized everyone must be asleep and so she returned to her bedroom, turned off the light and crawled into bed.

It was the worst night's sleep she'd ever gotten. She guessed she may have slept peacefully for 2 out of the six hours that she laid there. She couldn't remember what happened in her sleep, but it didn't matter right now. She could smell breakfast and coffee. She got dressed quickly. Threw on some jeans and a baggy t-shirt. She knew she'd be doing something outside today. At least she hoped she would. She grabbed her notebook and the book about who and what she thought she was, ran down the stairs and collided straight into Shawn. Shawn was the neighbor, and her lifelong best friend. He was a large muscular man around her age. Spending days on his farm had made him tan and his blue eyes sparkled like the sea.

"Holy Shit Shawn! I wasn't sure I'd get to see you this weekend." She wrapped her arms around him and gave him a squeeze.

"Who are you and what have you done with my little flower?!" He questioned her while eyeing her up and down. She felt her face heat up. It wasn't because of the little flower comment. He'd called her that since they were children. It was the way he was looking at her, all of her.

"It's me you big ogre!" She teased him. "I've just changed that's all."

"I'll say. Sorry I didn't stop yesterday to wish you a happy birthday. Some of the sheep got out and it took me damn well all day and night to wrangle those dumb asses back onto the property."

"Why didn't you come get us? It would have gone so much faster with five more bodies helping."

"And be on the hook for ruining your birthday dinner? No thanks! I like the way my balls feel not in my throat."

'I'd like your balls down my throat.' Mellie thought. *'What the actual fuck is happening to me?! Balls in my throat?!!!! Thank God, I didn't say it out loud.'*

"Earth to Mellie!!! I was just kidding. I just knew it was the first time you'd seen your dad and grandpa in a while, and I wanted you to enjoy it."

"Thank you for thinking of me, but I can assure my birthday wouldn't have been ruined."

"Awww you really do love me."

Mellie blushed and looked away. Bashfully she said," Hey, you wanna stay for breakfast?"

"I can't, sadly. I have to take one of my girls to the vet. She fell while they were out last night and she's pregnant. Want to make sure the little one is ok." Shawn said. "But, how about you and I grab dinner tonight?

Birthday dinner two on me."

"Sure, I'd love to." She gave him a quick hug before he walked out the door. She would have to go shopping; she had nothing dinner appropriate to wear. But first, breakfast and talk about the Eternal Lady.

"So, dinner date?" Aileen asked as she set the rest of the food on the table.

"So, dinner date. What did I just agree to?" She was shocked that this is how her mother was seeing this dinner.

"Mellie, that young man has been pining over you since you were just his little flower. He's a good guy so go out and enjoy yourself." Callum said with an enormous grin on his face.

"Ok Dad, but first…. I think I know what I am. At least the basics. I finished the book you two have never needed to read."

"Ok Love, let's get our food and then we can talk. Grandpa and I are both very eager to hear what you've learned."

They all loaded their plates with eggs, sausage, bacon and fried potatoes. A big bowl of fresh fruit was passed around, along with coffee, milk and fresh squeezed orange juice. The biscuits came out last and they were the biggest and freshest Mellie thought she'd ever seen.

As they started to eat Mellie opened her notebook and began.

"So, I know you've all heard about the Eternal Lady. At least I know you used to tell me stories about her. I always thought it was a fairy tale, but it's not. She Is where our family tree started. I know that because the book goes back 200 years and that's where the family tree starts. Dad, she's your forever ago great grandmother. She was the original Wulver. That part I'm still trying to understand. She had powers that made her shape shift, but not just into a wolf. She could become any animal she needed to be at that moment. No human shifting that I've read so far.

"Mellie said as she shoveled food into her mouth.

"That's what we were thinking. We knew there had been someone else that was unlike the men in our family. The only guess was her as we can't go any further back than her. Also dear… I know how good it feels to eat like your life depends on it, especially when it's this new, but try not to eat like that when you're at dinner. I know Shawn wouldn't care, but everyone around you two may."

She gently smacked her dad on the arm and continued.

"So, as I discovered on the family tree, you are the first son to only have a daughter. So naturally I'm the only person that this "gift" could be passed down to or else it would die with you Dad. I don't know what it is that you two do exactly, but I know it's important."

"We'll take you out tomorrow and show you some of what we do."

"Ok, so here's my biggest find. The very last page of the book said one thing. Just one sentence. 'She will be reborn when she is needed'

That's it. That's the last thing in the book."

Her parents and grandparents looked back and forth for what seemed like eternity. Then her dad put his hand on her shoulder and squeezed.

"Tomorrow, we will take you with us and tell you what we've lived and everything we know. Today you read a couple more of those books and write down any questions. First, take your mother and grandmother to help find you something to wear to dinner." He kissed the top of her head, and the men walked outside.

"Ladies," Mellie said, "Bring me the dishes. Once this mess is cleaned up, we'll go shopping. I need your help. I don't know what will look ok on this new body."

"Everything. Literally anything you wear will look good. But let's do it!" Aileen said.

"Let's shop till we drop!" agreed Amelia

Her grandmother loved to spend money. After the farm it was her greatest joy. Of course usually she was shopping for baking ingredients, or feed for the animals.

CHAPTER SEVEN

They jumped into Mellie's car and headed to town. It was a scenic drive through the hill side, and for the first time ever Mellie was interested in all of it. The grass was a dark emerald green. The most beautiful wildflower fields surrounded them in every color imaginable. Mellie didn't love the fact that it was incredibly overcast. It was better than the alternative. Droughts made it hard for the neighboring crops to grow. So the rain was the best option.

They arrived at the center of town, parked and started walking to the shops. There were a ton of shops to look at, but there weren't many plus size stores and that, now more than ever, is what she needed. Her main priority was to find something sweet and appropriate for a birthday dinner with Shawn. She was nervous and she wasn't sure why. She had known him her whole life so this shouldn't be a big deal. However, the knowledge that he'd had a thing for her for years had changed something in her. He was, in her mind, the dream man. He was tall and stood no shorter than 6'4", He had the dreamiest sky like blue eyes, shoulder length brown hair and the perfect amount of facial hair. She hadn't seen him shirtless since they were in high school swimming at the lake over a holiday. But she knew the way his shirts sat on his chest that he was what she referred to as furry, and she hoped to see it one day. She had never allowed herself to think of him in these ways or at least not to this extent, so this was new territory.

They arrived at the perfect shop. Radiant Rose Apparel was a store that Mellie had never thought of walking into. It was the only store near her that sold girly plus size clothing that could be considered sexy. She had never wanted anyone to think of her this way, so it wasn't something that ever crossed her mind. When they entered the store, she gazed longingly at the dresses all around her. There were dresses in all styles, lengths and colors. Thankfully the store was separated by color, so she knew exactly where she didn't want to look. That left her with anything in black, burgundy or emerald green. She went for the black as it had always slimmed her down, but her mom and grandmother walked straight to the section that held the green dresses. She wasn't sure about green, but she decided to give it a try. She let Amelia and Aileen grab anything they wanted her to try. Mellie still wasn't used to this body and had no clue what would even look remotely good on her. She impatiently waited in the fitting room. The ladies brought back an armful for her to try on. The first one Mellie picked up was a gorgeous grass green wrap dress that was just above the knee and had a deep V-neck. She questioned the choice instantly, wondering what they were thinking. But everything changed when she slipped the dress over her head.

She hated the color and the sleeves instantly but everything else was perfection. It was too hot and muggy for long sleeves. She walked out of the fitting room and Amelia and Aileen's mouths dropped. Before they started to speak, she said, "I love the way it looks. Mostly. However, I hate the color and the sleeves. I'm going to try some of the emerald dresses on." She turned around and walked straight back into the mountain of choices.

She rummaged through the dresses and stopped instantly when she saw what she already knew would be the one. It was green with black roses embroidered all over it. Not a wrap dress but just about the same length as the last one. It had a much deeper V and an A-line skirt. When she slipped it over her head she started to cry. She had never felt or looked so beautiful in her life. She got up the nerve and dried the tears streaming down her cheeks. She slowly walked out and presented herself to the most important women in her life, and Blair. Unknown to her Amelia had called Blair and there she stood. Her mouth was on the floor. Amelia and Aileen had also begun to cry.

"Oh Sweety," Blair exclaimed, "If you don't buy this right now it will be a disservice to anyone who sees you tonight, but especially to you." She walked over and hugged Mellie.

"I never thought I'd be able to look at myself and love what I see and want other people to notice it. I feel great! Blair, you better not take back the shopping spree idea!"

"Never love! Next Monday you're mine for the day!"

"Ok, go get dressed and let's get you ready." Mellie hustled into the dressing room and was out in a flash. She grabbed a simple pair of black strappy heels and headed to checkout. Another 45 minute drive and they pulled down the long drive and headed into the house. The guys were out in the fields, so the house was quiet when they walked in. Quiet aside from the Barley barking uncontrollably which hadn't stopped since he'd seen Mellie the day of her change. It wasn't a bad bark. No aggression in the tone. More like a, "What did you do to my

Mellie?" type of bark. Mellie headed to her room with Blair hot on her heels.

"Ok, we've got two hours until Shawn picks you up! Let's get to work." Blair yelled excitedly.

Blair had come prepared with her whole arsenal. Everything from makeup to hair tools to skin care. She knew that Mellie didn't really have a "skin care routine". That would have to change now. They started with hot rollers. Mellie had never worried much about her hair. Her go to style was to pull it back in a ponytail or a messy bun. Easy and simple. Today it would be down and curly. A strange concept for her simplistic style to grasp. When her hair was up and setting, Blair worked on Mellie's face. Blair didn't skip skin care ever and now Mellie wouldn't either. It was a torturous 12 step routine, but it felt really good. Then Blair started with the makeup. Mellie hadn't paid much attention to anything that was happening. She just sat down and enjoyed it, but she started to hear plastic crinkle. She looked over and realized everything that Blair had used on her was brand new.

"Blair, why are you using your brand new everything on me? I would have been more than ok with using your things." She said feeling kind of bad.

"They're not my things. Your mom called me last night. She told me about your date and so I started shopping after I ate dinner. It's all yours and you better use it everyday!" She laughed and started on Mellie's face again. When her makeup was finished Blair grabbed some gold jewelry, which unbeknownst to Mellie was also hers.

"Ok, Let's see what this hair looks like." Blair began to take down her hair and it fell in beautiful loose curls just past her shoulders.

"OMG girl, you look stunning! Now, go get dressed and DO NOT LOOK AT YOURSELF!!"

Mellie grabbed her new dress and shoes and walked behind her changing divider. She heard her door close and figured that Blair had run to the bathroom. When she was all dressed, she stepped out from behind the wall and heard gasps. Not only from Blair, but from everyone. Amelia, Aileen, Callum and Angus stood there with tears in their eyes.

"Mellie, sweety you look incredible." Her mom said with tears streaming down her face. Mellie slowly walked over to her wooden framed full length mirror. When she saw herself tears welled up in her eyes.

"I have always felt ok with myself. But, today, for the first time ever I love how I look. I hope it's not too different. I really hope Shawn likes my look."

"If he doesn't think you look breathtaking, he's blind." Her father said.

"Ok, we'll go downstairs. Blair stay with her and make sure she doesn't change her mind. We'll call you both down when he gets here."

The family weren't down there very long when they heard the front door open. Shawn walked in looking like a model off the pages of a magazine.

"He's here girls!" Called Aileen.

CHAPTER EIGHT

Mellie slowly walked down the stairs. When she saw Shawn she froze. He looked incredible. Not that he didn't look great all the time but tonight he was different. He was wearing black slacks, with black suede boots and a deep blue button up shirt. Mellie was so used to seeing him in jeans, tee, and work boots that she didn't know how to react. He slowly walked towards her and gave her his hand. She hit the landing and he promptly spun her around like they were dancing.

"You've never looked more lovely my little flower." He said as he spun her slowly one more time.

"You clean up pretty nice yourself ogre. You smell wonderful." They stood there staring at each other like they were the only two in the room.

"Alright you two. Get out of here and enjoy your night!" Callum said as he ushered them out the door. They walked up to Shawn's black lifted Chevy Silverado. He took her hand, opened the door and helped her inside. She didn't have a clue where he was taking her and quite frankly, she didn't care.

As they hit the highway, she hadn't a clue as to where they were going. It didn't really matter. Outside of the two or three tiny town cafes she wasn't use to eating out. Especially at a fancy restaurant. Anywhere worth a celebration was 45 minutes away. While not super far, for farm workers it was a bit inconvenient. They got off the exit and Mellie knew exactly where he was taking her. Johnny's bar. A Northern Italian restaurant that opened in the 1820's. It was the perfect place for any celebration. Shawn had taken her there once before. The day she graduated college. He had taken her there and she hadn't been able to eat at any chain Italian restaurant since. They walked in and her senses overwhelmed her. The temperature was perfect. The wonderful classical music was playing at the perfect volume. She could smell everything together yet separate. Seafood, sauces and oh the garlic! She couldn't wait to dig in. Shawn walked up to the hostess and told her his name. They were promptly led into the kitchen. Set off in one corner was a booth. She looked at him like he was crazy.

"Why are we back here?" she asked.

"I figured we could sit here by ourselves and have a real conversation. Plus, I have one more surprise for you after our main course. That surprise only comes with the kitchen table reservation." Shawn explained.

"I'm excited but also a bit nervous. Not to mention I can't imagine how much this cost you. Thank you so much."

Shawn pulled out a chair for Mellie. He gently placed his hand on her shoulder as we walked to his side of the table. It gave Mellie chills. This is the first time she'd ever felt this special. To also feel this beautiful at the same time was something she had never experienced.

They weren't handed a food menu. Only one for their drinks. She thought it was odd but didn't say anything. After they received their drinks, the chef walked up to their table and handed them what she would come to learn was the 1st of 7 courses. The first thought that popped into her head was how much had this cost Shawn?.... She had a way of thinking anything good that came to her was not warranted or even deserved. The first course was a wonderful loaf of crispy bread with a garlic olive dipping oil. Every drop was wonderful. They had light conversation. Just talking about their everyday lives. How things were going at the farm and the magazine. They drank a glass of red wine while they were eating and talking. The chef then brought them each a small bowl of Italian wedding soup. The dish was so light and comforting.

Mellie was having the time of her life just eating and watching the kitchen staff at work. They were so fast and efficient. After their soup a sous chef brought out their salad. It was a wonderful Tuscan artichoke tomato salad. There was a light vinaigrette on top with some freshly made croutons. They were still warm. They were the perfect blend of soft and crunchy at the same time. While they were eating their salads Shawn took a deep breath and set a small wrapped package on the table.

"I wanted to make sure I got you something that you would love as well as the dinner. I have so much I want to say to you and I'm afraid if I don't do it now I'll chicken out and may not get the chance."

This made Mellie's stomach flip and she got kind of nervous. Maybe not nerves, but excitement. They often felt the same to her. She felt her face warm.

He started slowly. "Mellie, why don't you open your gift first, and then I can let you know my heart?" He slipped the package across the table. When Mellie reached over to accept it, their fingers touched, and she felt butterflies in her stomach.

Mellie carefully unwrapped the box. When she opened the box a small velvet jewelry box came out. She slowly opened the box. Her whole face lit up and tears filled her eyes. He had bought her a wonderful gold necklace with a small bunch of sunflowers. There was a small bee sitting on one of the petals. She turned the pendant over and found her initials and his on the back. She looked up at him and slowly reached out to take his hand.

"I don't know what to say. It's the most beautiful thing I've ever seen." She said while moving her gaze between him and the necklace. "Will you put it on me?"

Shawn slowly stood up and walked around the table. He gently moved the hair from her neck and placed it over her left shoulder. This made Mellie's whole body quiver. She wanted to be closer to him, so she laid her head back, so it was laying against his firm stomach. She looked up into his eyes and he leaned down and softly kissed her forehead.

"I'm so glad you like it. I made it with only you in mind, my little flower." He clasped the necklace closed and lightly squeezed her hand as he walked back to his side of the table

"You made it? That makes it even more special. I'll wear it always."

She knew Shawn had picked up a new hobby. This must have been it. she said as she bent down and kissed the fingers that were wrapped around hers.

"I don't know when this happened, but I need to tell you how I feel. I think it's always been a thing, but I was too shy and nervous to say anything. Especially when you moved to the city. I didn't want to stop your dreams and make you feel trapped. Mellie, I've always wanted to be in your life. I can't seem to be around you enough. I want you to be mine. I've fallen in love with you sometime in our life."

"I don't know how. You have always been in my life. I needed to be invisible. I knew we were friends and never dreamed of anything more. You are so perfect and I'm just me. Forever trying to be invisible. I never thought I was special enough to be on your radar." Mellie laid all her insecurities out.

"Don't be silly. You've always been the one for me. I was always too nervous to say anything because I could tell you weren't interested."

"Weren't interested? I've always, and I mean ALWAYS, had the most intense crush on you. I just didn't want to be let down if you were only in it for friendship. Which, rest assured, would have been fine."

"So, Mellie, do you think we can give this a shot? A couple of dates while you're here. Just to see what happens? If we're not compatible which just isn't possible or if you get bored, we can just go back to the way things were before."

She wrapped her left hand tightly around his and with her right touched her necklace. "I'd be more than willing to give this a try. Just know with all the changes that have happened recently I'm not sure where the autumn will take me. When I can talk about it you will be the first to know."

"Naturally", Shawn laughed.

They had gotten very comfortable and she finally let the nerves go.

The wine was flowing and they talked about everything. Work, family, Mellie talked about all the fun things she'd gotten into at work and how she had officially taken a remote job. She'd only be going into the office once a month if she couldn't get out of it. She told him some crazy Blair stories, and they just shook their heads and laughed. He talked about his parents and how the farm was doing great and had become very self-sustaining. He let her know about his friend Jack and how he had just started dating a new girl and how she was the one. Shawn hadn't met her yet, but based on the change in Jack he believed it.

The server cleaned off the table, brought out some water and then served their seafood option. A lovely plate of lemon butter scallops served over Orzo. The meal had finally come to the half way point. It was amazing. Mellie loved how they left enough time between portions that they hadn't grown full. Not that she would with her newfound appetite. She hadn't let Shawn see that side of her tonight. At least she hoped that she hadn't.

The next dish they brought out was a wonderful-looking and aromatic chicken Sorrentino. The chicken was moist, tender and cooked to perfection. When they had finished their main course the chef walked up to them.

"Now, it's time for the two of you to come with me." Shawn hopped up so excited. Mellie, on the other hand looked confused but got up and walked with them to another room. She was confident it was where the desserts were made. Chef handed them each an apron and led them to the sink so they could wash up.

"Tonight, you will help me make your desserts. You'll be making two desserts tonight on a small scale so you can eat both. First a wonderful common cannoli, and then we'll be making a zeppole."

Mellie's eyes began to sparkle. One of her favorite things to do in the world was to create desserts for her mother and grandmother.

"Oh, Shawn, this will be wonderful. Officially the best night ever!

Maybe we can make enough to share with our parents when we go home!" "That's an amazing idea! Hey, Chef, do you think that's something we could do?"

"Absolutely! Let's get to work."

They worked hard and fast to create the most beautiful Italian pastries they had ever tried. They placed two of each on a plate for them to share and then boxed the rest up evenly to take to their homes.

They took their plate to their table and the server brought out two small espressos. Mellie bit into the cannoli and moaned out in pleasure. Shawn's face grew red and then he took his own bite and let out a moan of pleasure as well. Mellie didn't blush, she laughed uncontrollably which made him follow suit. They talked and savored their dessert and coffee. When they were finished a string trio walked up to the table and started to play an incredible lovely and romantic song.

Shawn held out his hand to Mellie, "Would you like to include our first dance in tonight's festivities?"

"Without a doubt. But I may never want to leave your arms."

"That could be arranged. Aside from the drive home. That may be dangerous." Shawn laughed.

He held out his hand and gently led her into the middle of the floor. They started to dance and gradually got closer until his arms fully enveloped her and she could lay her head against his firm yet soft chest. They danced through at least four songs. It felt like they were only dancing for a second. The band stopped and she glanced up at Shawn. He leaned his head down and gently brushed his lips against hers. She left out a soft sigh and laid her head once again on his chest. They slowly made their way back to the table where a cheese and fruit tray lay. A bottle of brandy and two stunning brandy glasses.

When they finally finished dinner, they picked up their boxed desserts and slowly walked out the door hand in hand. He walked her to her door and opened it. When he got into the truck she moved into the middle seat buckled in and laid her head on his shoulder as he drove home. He pulled down her drive and nudged her awake.

"I'm so sorry I fell asleep. I must have been more tired than I thought."

"That brandy did you in." He chuckled. "Let me walk you to the door.

Don't forget the dessert."

She grabbed the box and his hand. They slowly walked to the door. She looked up and put her free hand on the back of his head and pulled him down for a kiss. He kissed her gently on the lips and they heard an audible "awwwwww" coming from inside the house.

"Oh my God, Oh my God!!!!" She turned fifty shades of red.

"It's ok Mellie. They already knew this was going to happen."

"Maybe, but this is the first time they've ever seen anything like this from me."

"They're happy for us. I promise." He leaned down and pecked her on the lips one more time. "Goodnight and I'll call you tomorrow."

"Goodnight Shawn. Sleep well." She slowly walked into the house, ready to face the firing squad.

"Looks like you had a good night." Her mom said. "Did it go as well as we hoped it would?"

"Not sure what you were hoping for, but it went well. Very well. We ate, drank, he gave me this wonderful gift that HE MADE, we talked, and we made desserts for everyone! I am, however, very tired and need to go to bed. I'll see everyone in the morning."

Mellie walked up the stairs quickly as to not be bombarded with any more questions. When she entered her room, she lay down on her bed and let out a great sigh. She placed her hand on her necklace and thought about what an amazing night it had been. She decided to text Shawn goodnight. "Goodnight. Thank you for tonight and I'll see you tomorrow."

"Sleep well my flower and I'll see you in the morning."

She closed her eyes and started to drift asleep. Her eyes shot open, she hopped off her bed and ran downstairs.

"DAD, GRANDPA, how do I do this with someone in my life?!"

"Slow down. First know that you will be able to tell your mate, your family and a trusted friend. You can't go through this alone and you shouldn't have to. We can talk about it more in the morning before Shawn gets here. You're a ways off from that, so don't worry."

"I was almost asleep, and the thought just popped into my head. I had to ask, and I had to ask right now. I'm going to try to go back to bed now. I love you all." Mellie walked back up the stairs and changed into her favorite "grandma" nightgown. She drifted happily asleep.

CHAPTER NINE

When Mellie woke up the next day, she wasn't sure what to expect but she did know what she was about to do. She could smell the bacon, eggs, and coffee wafting through the air. She put on her robe and headed downstairs. Everyone was sitting around the table except for Dad who was cooking. She had never seen that before. She sat down at the table and her mom brought her a hot cup of coffee and a glass of orange juice. Just as they were about to eat someone knocked on the door.

"Oh, that must be Shawn!" Grandma exclaimed. She got up and opened the door. Sure enough, Shawn stood there in all his splendor. Back in his everyday farm attire and a bouquet of flowers, or two that he had picked from the wildflowers growing in between their properties. He handed the smaller bouquet to Grandma with a hug and walked over to Mellie. He lay the flowers on the table next to her, bent down, and kissed her forehead lightly.

She was beaming. "Thank you, Shawn. Sit and join us for breakfast. Dad's been "Cooking" all day." She looked at him worriedly. Her dad didn't have the best reputation for his cooking.

Shawn took the seat next to Mellie and mom brought him a black coffee and a glass of OJ. They talked about the day's plans as they ate.

"I'll be working on the new stall so it's ready when we get our new girl." Mellie told them excitedly.

"I'll be sheering sheep all morning. Then I plan on taking Mellie on a ride and a picnic for lunch. Shawn looked at her like he was asking and also telling her.

"Go ahead! Work on the stall a bit and then we can handle the rest. Work around here is fast-moving when our guys are home." Amelia was encouraging this to work out and Mellie wasn't angry about it at all.

When breakfast was over Mellie got dressed and headed straight outside. She had the window installed and the gate up faster than she had ever worked before. She was back in the house, changing into something cute yet practical well before noon. She had just got her shoes on and was headed outside to saddle her horse when Shawn walked out of the barn with Bonnie. He walked towards his horse and waited for her to join him. He had loaded up a sidesaddle with what Mellie could only assume was lunch.

"Hey Clyde", Mellie sweetly patted the stallion on the head. Yes, Clyde. They had received their horses at the same time. Ten years ago, they had named them together. They knew it was a little cheesy, but now it kind of fit perfectly.

"Where are we headed!?" asked Mellie with pure excitement in her voice.

"I was exploring the public park nearby, and I'm pretty sure you'll love it. It's secluded and it's the perfect place for a picnic."

They hopped on their horses and took the quick five-mile ride to the park. They rode down a small man-made path surrounded by dense trees. Then they came to a small clearing that was full of the sweetest smelling blackberry bushes she had ever seen.

"Ooooo, can we stop and pick some before we continue?"

"Of course, Mellie. This day is about you." Shawn told her.

"It's also about you, and I wasn't sure if you were in a time crunch."

"My whole day is yours. I know you have to get back to work tomorrow. Even though you'll be home I know you'll be busy."

"Then my day is yours. Let's stop and get some of these berries. They'll be great for dessert." What Mellie didn't know was that Shawn had planned it that way. He had brought shortcake and freshly made whipped cream so they could have blackberry shortcake after their dinner picnic. He had planned the entire day, and he couldn't wait to see it all unfold.

When they came out of another set of trees the river lay before them. It was stunning. Flat rocks lined both sides of the river. Perfect for sun bathing, picnicking and even slanting ones that were perfect for sliding into the water on days when cooling off was a necessity. Before Mellie knew what hit her Shawn was hopping off his horse and handing her the reins. He pulled his shirt over his head and Mellie got a wonderful glimpse of his fur covered chest. He was muscular but not overly so. He had the perfect amount of padding over his muscles, but they were still noticeably there. He ran down to the river and covered the slanting rock as best as he could with water.

"What are you doing?!" screamed Mellie with childish excitement.

"It's hot and I need to cool off! Come on. Get on in here."

Mellie let him slide down the rock and laughed until she couldn't breathe. She missed having fun like this with Shawn. It was so different now. He wasn't a little boy anymore. He was the perfect specimen of a man, and hers. Mellie decided to keep her shorts on but slipped out of her shoes and slowly and self-consciously slipped her shirt over her head.

When she pulled the shirt off her eyes Shawn was just standing there, in the river, looking at her like she was some sort of delicious treat. She blushed and walked towards the rock slide. She took a deep breath and slid down the rock head first. When she stood up our of the water she was laughing and had the biggest smile he'd seen in a while. That is of course the night before when he'd kissed her.

She walked towards him with a seductive stare. He met her in the middle, closed his eyes, leaned down and kissed her lips. She was perfect. When he opened his eyes, she had a mischievous look on her face. Then she splashed him exuberantly. He grabbed her around the waist and kissed her thoroughly.

"Come on beautiful, let's eat. There's another place more secluded that I want you to see." They sat down on the blanket and Shawn got the food out while Mellie slipped her shirt back on.

He had packed the perfect spread. Sandwiches on french bread, a wonderful salad, strawberries, watermelon and apples all clean cute and ready to eat. Then he pulled out a bottle and two wine glasses. Mellie knew what it was instantly. His father's famous strawberry wine that he made from the strawberries they grew every year on the farm. Then he pulled out a covered wicker bowl and a glass dish holding what looked like whipped cream.

"Mom made us some shortcake and whipped cream. I figure now that we've picked blackberries, we can use them or the strawberries I brought for dessert." Shawn said with a giant smile on his face.

"You've thought of everything haven't you?"

"I tried, I hope I got it right." Shawn said looking a little self-conscious.

Mellie put her hand on his, "You have nothing to worry about," she said," We know almost everything about each other. You can't mess this up." She leaned in and gently kissed his perfect lips.

Shawn stood up and quickly slipped his shirt over her head. He was every bit as perfect as Mellie remembered.She quickly looked away when he pulled his shirt over his head. He saw her anyway and knew exactly what she was looking at. The next thing she knew he was walking into the river in his socks and shorts.

"What are you doing crazy?!"

"I'm having fun. Come join me. She watched him as he began to throw water on a rock that she was sure would become a slide. She watched him walk back out of the water, and she was right. He sat down on that rock and slid all the way down. She laughed at his as she pulled her shirt over her head. When she looked at him again, he was staring at her. She instantly became self-conscious and covered herself up with her hands.

"Don't you dare cover up that perfect body. I want to admire every inch of you." Shawn said with confidence and love. She slowly uncovered herself and looked down at him with her face glowing red.

She walked to the slide and slid down with a girlish giggle. When she got out of the water, he was standing there looking at her. She didn't know what to do, so, true to her fashion she spun around and splashed him. The next thing they knew they were laughing the way they did when they were kids. They played in the water for what seemed like forever. They would have stayed there all day, until he heard her stomach growl.

"Come on lovely lady. Let's get something to eat." Shawn said.

"As much fun as I'm having that sounds like a great idea." They got out of the water and walked over to their blanket and food. He had brought all the right things. There were sandwiches with all the fixings, a cheese plate and so much fruit. They ate to their hearts content and then he pulled out a basket of vanilla shortcakes and fresh whipped cream. He then took out the blackberries they had picked and some strawberries he has soaking in sugar. They ended up not eating the cakes. They were too full, but never too full for berries and cream.

He took a strawberry, dipped it in the cream and touched it to her nose before he gently fed it to her. She tried to be smooth, but smooth she was not. Her attempt to look sexy while being fed turned into something that made him laugh so much that he choked on the blackberry he had been eating. Embarrassment turned into laughter when he leaned over and kissed her, covering his nose with cream. When they had sufficiently stuffed themselves, he laid back. She followed suit and laid in the crook of his still shirtless arm. She placed her head gently on his chest. They just lay there staring at the clouds. She placed her hand on his chest and started running her fingers through his chest hair. With no notice he moaned, and she pulled away quickly.

"You didn't have to quit. I was enjoying that very much." He grabbed her hand softly kissed the tips of her fingers and placed them back on his chest. They both drifted off to sleep. When they woke up the sun was high in the afternoon sky. She started packing up the picnic. "Here, let me help you. It'll go faster and then we can spend more time at our next destination."

"Wait! There's somewhere else on the agenda?"

"Yes, and I don't think even you have been there." Shawn laughed. She had been such an outdoorsy person he wasn't sure if there was any part of the neighboring three towns that she hadn't seen, but he was hopeful she'd missed this gem. He'd only seen it once on a solo run about a week ago, so he was confident that it was something she hadn't yet seen.

They finished packing up and hopped on Bonnie and Clyde. The next thing Mellie knew they were riding through the river to get to the other side. In fact, she had never been to the other side of the river, and every second she was getting more and more excited. When they hit the bank on the other side, he took a right and started riding alongside the river. Then he veered right into a place that wasn't much of a path at all but seemed like something that they could do. They again rode deeper into the woods when finally, he hopped down and tied Clyde to a tree. She followed suit.

They made their way around a giant oak tree, and her jaw dropped to the floor. Before her there was a wonderful reservoir surrounded by those giant flat rocks. The trees were bright green and kept the grove hidden. When she was only thinking about stripping naked and jumping in Shawn was doing that exact thing. Her eyes went wide when she followed his chest down to his hip bones. She turned around before her eyes veered further down and he chuckled.

"Get in and close your eyes, and I'll jump in to."

After a couple of excruciatingly long minutes, he heard a splash. He then felt her arms around his waist. He opened his eyes and slowly trailed his gaze down to the middle of her chest, right where the water hit. Shawn in turn wrapped his arms around her waist and held her close while his lips found hers. It started as a normal warm loving kiss but quickly flared into a kiss full of passion. His hands trailed up her side and his thumbs gently brushed the sides of her breasts. Her breath hitched and she leaned into it. She started running her fingers through his chest hair again all while their kiss continued. Before they had gotten in, he had laid the picnic blanket on one of the rocks. Somewhere for them to lay down and dry off. He lifted her out of the water and placed her on the blanket. She wrapped the blanket around herself and laid on her side watching him in the water. He seemed nervous to get out.

"Give me a second and I'll spread the blanket, so you have a place to lay." She then turned around to hide herself but to also give him space to get out of the water without being watched.

She felt his wet body touch her back and his hands wrap around her. He gently laid his hands on her lower stomach and then rubbed his thumb in gentle circles until she moaned. She turned her head to the side and lowered his lips to hers. As they passionately kissed his hand ran up her midsection and stopped right under her left breast. His thumb sweeping back and forth right under her nipple. It made her sigh and shiver at his touch. She arched her back to kiss him further and he felt her ass against his ever-growing erection. When he tried to back away, she placed her left arm on his thigh.

"Please don't move. I love the feel of you." She pushed back even further and rocked her ass back and forth. She deepened their kiss once again, turning over. She looked up at him with desire in her eyes. She pecked him once more on the lips.and then slowly moved down kissing his jaw line, ear and neck.

"Please be careful Mellie. You're going to drive me crazy."

"What if that's my intention?" She said, looking at him mischievously. She placed her hands on his chest and ran them down the entire length of his torso. She reached what, in her mind she called the pleasure patch, and grinned up at him. She started rubbing down his chest and got to the place right below the belly button and licked her way all the way to the base of his shaft. She looked up to her with desire and need in her eyes.

"Get up here, sexy, my turn." She instantly got nervous. "Love don't be nervous. You are the only person I've ever wanted, and I want all of you. Now lay back." Shawn looked down at her before slowly lowering his head to the nape of her neck. He started to lightly kiss, lick and suck his way down her neck. When his mouth reached her left nipple, she inhaled sharply and let out a quiet passionate moan. He stayed there for simultaneously what seemed like a second and an hour. She wanted him to stay right there but also wanted him to run his mouth over her incredibly wet center. He slowly continued down her torso. Peppering wet kisses and seductively licking his way down to her pleasure point. Her eyes shot open when his lips disappeared from her body.

"Hey you, where'd you go? Please keep touching me!" Mellie cried.

"I wouldn't dream of stopping I'm just changing directions." Shawn said and she looked down and he was between her feet. She was also so so glad that she had shaved all the important parts. Especially since all this extra hair had started to appear all over her body. She moaned with pure pleasure when he began to kiss and lick up her legs. When Shawn reached her knees, he put a hand just above the knees and spread her legs. The entire time she was so drowned in pleasure that she didn't take even an instant to feel self-conscious or unsure of her body. He began to kiss up her inner thighs. When he reached the bend between her hip bone and her mound, he took a deep breath in and moaned. When he blew out the air touched her sweet spot, and he could not only hear the pleasure that it brought her. He could also smell and see the pleasure it gave. He placed his hands on her inner thighs placing his thumbs in the perfect spot to run his fingers along her folds and gently circled her clit with his thumbs. She had never been cared for this much, especially in the sex arena. It had always been a give and don't get kind of situation, and she was drinking up every second of attention. She could feel her body tremble and had never wanted anything more than she wanted this man in this moment. She laid there loving every second and then she felt a finger entering her and she quit breathing as he entered another finger into her. Her body started to quiver.

"Please keep going. I'm going to cum."

"I intend to make you cum so much today that you'll beg me to stop. Just lay back and enjoy." Her body started shaking as her first orgasm soared through her and she cried out in pleasure. He pulled his fingers out, licked and sucked on them and made a noise that let her know he liked the way she tasted. The next thing she knew she felt his tongue reaching for her most secret areas. She had never had anyone taste her so intimately. It didn't take long before she was well on her way to climax again. As the intensity built, she started to shake and then he felt her muscles tight around his tongue and his mouth flooded with her juices. She tasted amazing and he couldn't get enough.

"Please come up here I need a break."

"Ok, but it won't last long. I'll give you a minute to catch your breath and then you'll be seeing stars again." Shawn said in a way that made her do a double take.

"You sure are confident, aren't you?" Mellie questioned.

"I just know I can please you and I can't stop wanting to make you moan." He laid down again and wrapped his arms around Mellie and pulled her into his side. She began running her hand up and down his chest again. As she continued her hand started to move further south until eventually her hand was in the right spot that he let out a small moan. She found herself wrapping her hand around the thick girth of his shaft and gently squeezing. He was so much bigger than she had anticipated and was both nervous and excited about that. He was lying there with his eyes closed enjoying the feeling. She spat on her hand and moistened him so that her hand moved with more ease. He deeply inhaled when she lightly breathed out onto his member.

"I've never felt this good getting pleasured." He sighed

"Oh, just wait. If you liked that you'll love this." She slowly got up and kneeled between his legs. She took his shaft in her hand once again. He watched as she opened her mouth and lowered her head to him. She began by licking the tip slowly while looking directly in his eyes. "Oh. My. God." He moaned. She knew she had him then. With no further playing around she took him into her mouth and with no warning was balls deep. He was still looking into her eyes as they began to roll into the back of her head. She slowly released him from her mouth and let the spit fall onto the tip of him. She began to lower her head again.

"No, stop. I want to finish with you. If you're comfortable with that."

"It's safe, I'm on birth control. We're both too busy to worry about body count. I just want to feel all of you inside of me." Her hand was still around his shaft and when she said that he twitched in her palm. She crawled up and straddled him. She slowly lowered herself onto him. When she started to open to him, she realized just how big he was. She looked down at him with seduction in her eyes and slid down the rest of his length. She saw his eyes roll back and heard him let out a low moan. Shawn reached up and cupped her breasts in his hands. He began to use his thumb and index finger to lightly pinch and pull on her swollen firm nipples. Mellie started to slowly rotate her hips and move rhythmically up and down. He pulled her down and kissed her passionately as she continued to move with him inside her. Without a second of warning, he flipped her over and held her legs in place so they wrapped more securely around his waist. He looked down at her and bit his lower lip. He then lowered his mouth to her left breast and lightly bit her nipple. She sucked in a breath and her nipple became even harder. He bit down a little harder and he began to thrust himself into her. With every thrust it got a little faster and a bit rougher.

"Please don't stop!" Mellie cried. "You feel so good inside me! Faster!!!." Shawn began to pound her perfect center, and she continued to beg for more. "I'm yours! Take me anyway you want!"

"Don't give me any ideas." Shawn purred. As he continued to pound into her sex her legs began to shake. He wanted them to finish together, so he slowed down a little, while keeping the strength of his thrusts. It didn't take him long and they were reaching their climax together. It was so strong that it lasted minutes. When they were spent, he stayed inside her and slipped back over so she was on top of him. She laid her head on his chest and enjoyed every second.

After they had laid there for a couple minutes his eyes shot open as she slowly began to rotate herself on him again. Mellie had never been this crazed for someone's body, but she needed him again, and all of him. This time was fast and ended quickly, but that's only because the sun was setting and the park would be closing soon.

"We better get dressed and head out of here or we'll be stuck all night." Mellie chuckled and began to stand up.

"I wouldn't mind that at all." Shawn said as he tried to pull her back down.

"As much as I'd love to, my parents will have a search party out here looking for us if we don't get home soon."

"I know you're teasing but I can actually see that happening," Shawn laughed. "Let's get out of here."

They begrudgingly got up and got their clothes on, grabbed their blanket and headed to the horses. As they headed home, they rode side by side and held hands as they went. In no time flat, which was far too soon, they were in Mellie's barn putting Bonnie away for the night.

"Good girl. Thanks for letting us enjoy our day." Mellie said as she gave Bonnie a special treat.

When she stepped out of the stall Shawn grabbed her and kissed her tight. "Do I get a special treat too?"

"I think you've gotten a few special treats today," Mellie teased as she kissed him fiercely. He pulled her close and wrapped his arms tightly around her. His hands found their way down and he cupped her ass in his hands.

"I need more of you already. Look at what you've done to me." He said as he guided her hand down to his ever growing erection.

"I don't think we'll ever get enough of each other." She said as she slowly undid his pants and freed him. She slowly got to her knees and took him into her mouth.

Neither one of them had ever gotten into this type of thing in a barn, but they were willing to give it a try. She began playing with his balls as she sucked and licked him until Shawn brought her back to a standing position.

"Let's go up to the loft. The hay is mostly soft, and it'll keep the horses from freaking out. Probably." Shawn said softly as he began rubbing her mound outside of her shorts.

"Sound's like a good idea." She barely got out between all the kisses. They walked over to the ladder, and he let her go first. She made it a point to go slowly and wiggle a little in front of him, so he got the whole picture as to what was going to happen. When Mellie reached the top of the ladder, she felt Shawn put his hand on her ass and propelled her the rest of the way up. It sent chills down her spine. She hopped up and quickly began taking her clothes off. By the time he hit the loft she was naked and standing there just gazing at him. His jaw hit the floor.

"I know that I have already seen all of you and felt all of you, but I'll never get tired of the view." Shawn said while slowly stripping down. He walked towards her with his eyes scrolling up and down. Drinking in every inch of her.

He got close enough and wrapped his arms around her waist. Mellie wrapped hers around his neck. He lifted her in the air then gently laid her down in the hay. The ends of each piece started to tickle her back side, but in the best way. She giggled.

"Hey, what are you laughing at?"

"This hay is tickling me. I like the way it feels." Mellie said while she continued to giggle.

"Oh really?" Shawn reached over, grabbed a small handful of hay. He slowly knelt between her legs and began to kiss his way down to her center. When he reached her honey pot he began to tease her with his tongue. He took the hay in his right and began to gently brush the pieces over her breasts. Mellie sucked in a big breath.

"Please keep doing it" She sighed. Shawn began to kiss his way up her belly while continuing to tease her with the hay. When he got to the perfect spot, he ran the hay up and down her legs as he entered her.

"Oh, God…. that feels incredible." He continued to push into her.

"Mmmmm. You're so deep."

"Oh, you sexy woman. It's not all I have to give you." Shawn growled and pushed into her even further. Mellie let out a scream and came instantly. Her legs shook for minutes even after the climax had ended.

"Shawn…. I need more."

"I'll give you more." He said as he thrust into her again, deep and hard. "Now get on your knees. I want to see that ass as I pound you."

"Yes, Sir." She said as she got on all fours in front of him.

"Oh, baby, don't say that. You'll really drive me crazy."

"That is the point Sir." With the second Sir he gently smacked her ass. She let out a loud gasp of pure pleasure.

"Please, more."

"Oh, you like that." He smacked her again but harder. He heard her let out another gasp of pleasure. He took more hay in his hand and ran it over the cheek he had just smacked.

"Babe, if you don't stop that we'll never get dressed again." Mellie gasped as she was smacked again.

"Maybe that's the point." He said as he spread her cheeks and with one big thrust entered her again. "I want to make you scream. I don't care if we wake up the whole world. You are mine and I am yours, and I want everyone to know it." He smacked her again and she pushed herself back so all of him was inside of her sweetness. He dropped the hay and held her right where she was with force. He pushed into her further and then rotated his hips. Shawn let go of her hips and he began to pull out of her. She laid her head on the hay and grabbed the back of his thighs to hold him tightly to her so he couldn't slide out. Shawn wrapped his hands around her pony tail and lightly pulled her head back. It made her shiver with anticipation and he felt it.

"You like that, don't you kitten." Shawn whispered in her ear.

"More than you know."

"Oh, by the way your juices are flowing down your legs, I think I have some idea." Shawn slid out of her but left the tip in. He kept one hand on her hair and the other hand when around and cradled her neck. "By the time I'm done with you tonight everyone will know what we did." Then he thrust into her with all of his strength. The second he hit her deepest depths she came so hard she kept her hands on the ground. She laid her face on the hay again and began to pull away. Shawn thought he had hurt her and was just about to let go, when she pushed back onto him so hard that he began to shudder.

"Babe, I want to keep going, but if you do that again I'm going to explode." Shawn gasped.

"Maybe that's my intention. You're mine, It's not like it won't happen again." She chuckled and pulled forward. Almost to the point where he was out of her. Then without any warning she slammed back again. He let out a low grunt and her legs began to shake again. He started to pound her hard and faster with each thrust. When she hit her climax and her walls tightened around his girth he came as well. When they had both finished, he rolled over and she laid there with her head on the floor and her ass still up in the air. He used his right hand and slid it between her legs. When he touched her folds her legs shook again. He brought his hand up and put it to her mouth. She happily tasted herself and him. She sucked his fingers clean and his cock throbbed again. He let his hand find her pleasure again.

"Hang on. This can't be one way. Let me roll over." Mellie moaned. She laid on her back and her left hand found his erect penis. She began to smear their sex all over the head. She tightly pumped him, and he slip two fingers into her. They played with each other until her hips began to buck and she came again. All over Shawns hand. She got to her knees and put him into her mouth. She went so deep she could feel him in her throat. She used her hands to play with his balls, and she continued to rotate her head and tongue. She felt him grow even harder as he came down her throat. She swallowed every drop while looking into his eyes. He ran his fingers through her hair. When she started to stand up, she looked at him again and licked her lips.

"Oh, God… Don't do that. I won't stay limp for long." Shawn moaned.

She giggled. "You're an animal. I should probably go inside. I know they saw us put Bonnie away. I'm sure they'll ask a million questions I don't want to answer."

"Then why don't you just stay in here with me and we can sleep in the hay?" Shawn asked.

"As much as I want to, I need to talk to them tonight. We're supposed to be planning our camping trip. I want you to come with us. Is that something you'd be interested in?"

"Absolutely! It's been years since I've joined your family on their trip. Plus, it would give me a perfect excuse to sleep with you multiple nights in a row."

"I like how your mind works." Mellie said while zipping her shorts.

"Let me down first so I can watch that fine ass of yours again." Shawn teased.

"I wouldn't have it any other way." Mellie winked.

When they made their way out of the barn he grabbed Clyde, and they walked to the bottom of the steps.

"Mellie, these have been the best days of my life. You have no idea how long I've wanted to be with you in every way imaginable." Shawn confessed.

"Why didn't you tell me? I've wanted to be with you as long as I can remember." Mellie said.

"I was afraid you'd say no. Then I was afraid you'd say yes and that it would ruin our friendship. I see now how foolish I was. Loving you from afar sure wasn't easy."

"Love?" Mellie looked at him with questioning eyes.

"Yes Mel. Love. I have loved you for most of my life. I always knew it would be you. Don't feel obligated to say it to me now. Take your time. I'm not going anywhere." Shawn pecked her on the lips. As he began to walk away, they held hands until their fingertips couldn't even brush anymore.

"Hey Shawn! Me too. I may need a bit to say it but just know… me too. Goodnight. Text me when you get in."

"Of course I will, and that's good to know. We have a long time to get this figured out, and I'm a patient man." He started walking away, turned and saw her standing there in a happy daze. "Mel! You may want to get the hay out of your hair."

She laughed so hard her belly ached. "Thanks Shawn. You too by the way." Then she happily walked inside. When she closed the door, she turned around to four sets of eyes staring at her with knowing glances.

CHAPTER TEN

"**B**oy, it sure took you and Shawn a long time to put Bonnie up!" Her mother laughed while winking.

"Mom… could you not? I'm currently walking on clouds. No need for the crash landing."

"Alright sweetie. Head to bed. We have an early morning of camping trip planning."

"Sure Mom. I have a question about that, but I can ask you in the morning." Mellie slowly began to walk up the stairs. She took a quick shower and climbed into bed. She dozed off happy, exhausted and a little sore. Before she knew it her nose woke her up. The smell of coffee and bacon could never let her rest. She glanced over at the clock. 5:30am…. "You've got to be kidding me." Mellie got out of bed and threw on some shorts and a tank. Forgoing the under garments as it was already hot and humid. When she hit the bottom of the stairs, she saw Shawn sitting at the table right next to her spot.

"Good morning beautiful." Shawn said as she sat down next to him. He leaned over and gave her a gentle kiss on the cheek. She leaned into him with a smile on her face.

"Good morning to you too." She chuckled.

"Alright love birds. Break it up. Mellie, can you come help me set the table?" Her grandmother asked.

"On my way Granny." Mellie joked. Everyone laughed, as she never called her granny. When all the food was on the table and everyone had orange juice and coffee Mellie sat down. When they had all finished eating Mom got out her notebook to start planning the camping trip.

There was a lot of decision making back and forth. From the location to the duration to the driving arrangements and everything in between. They finally agreed to Hocking Hills in Southern Ohio. Once they had finished talking about food, they began discussing driving arrangements. This is what Mellie had been waiting for.

"Hey, this is the perfect time for me to ask a question. How would everyone feel if Shawn accompanied us?" Mellie asked hopefully.

Her dad looked between them and smiled. "We wouldn't have it any way."

Mellie and Shawn looked at each other with huge grins on their faces.

"Just like that summer when we were kids." Shawn said

"I hope it's not just the same." Mellie winked. Mellie couldn't believe how things had changed so much in a week. She was living in a completely different world, and she loved it.

"So, when are we headed out?" Her mom asked.

"Well," said her dad," I figure next weekend. That way we have a good month to do as much as we can."

"Sounds good to us." Said Grandma, looking at Grandpa as he agreed.

They finished up breakfast and the guys cleaned up. Then they all went off to do their work for the day. Shawn grabbed Mellie's hand.

"I can't wait to spend a month with you and the family. It's going to be amazing. I'm going to head home to tell Dad and get to work. I'll call you later. Maybe we can take a walk down to the pond."

"I'd love that. I haven't even had a chance to fish yet this summer."

"Then, let's make it a fishing date. We can bring dinner home for our families."

"If I catch anything." Mellie joked. Shawn laughed. There wasn't a summer when Mellie hadn't won the town's fishing tournament. She was arguably better than him.

She leaned up and kissed him on the lips." I'll see you after lunch then."

"See you soon. Go get to work. I don't want to get yelled at for distracting you."

Mellie worked the entire morning. She loved every minute of the farm, but man was she tired. When she got back to the house she jumped in the shower. When she was clean and smelling not like a pile of hay she opened her dresser drawers. She decided on a pair of running shorts over her favorite bathing suit. She threw a halter top on and sat down at her desk to edit an article that was sent to her this morning. It was a short article about how the clothes she wore in high school were back in style. It was written by her boss so she knew she wouldn't have much to do. Fifteen minutes later she emailed the edited article back to Fiona. When that was done, she hurried downstairs to pack a small lunch for the fishing date. It was nothing like the dinners Shawn had made and bought for her, but it would be fast and easy. That way they'd be sure to have time to catch as many fish as possible. No sooner was she done than she heard a tap on the door. Shawn walked in, walked to Mellie and wrapped his arms around her waist. Leaning down he gently kissed her lips.

"Alright babe, I have the rods and bait in the truck. Ready to head out?"

"Sure am. I just got a little lunch packed so we can eat before we start." She said as she packed up a cooler.

They got in the truck and headed to the border of their properties. There sat the pond that they swan and fished in their entire lives. They hopped out of the truck and unloaded. After they set their chairs out Mellie handed Shawn his lunch. They ate and chatted about their day and all the fun they were going to have on the camping trip.

"I'm honestly a bit nervous about my training starting." She confided in him.

"Don't worry. Your grandpa and dad know what they're doing. I will also be right beside you. You'll do lovely." Shawn encouraged her in ways she'd never been before. With him she felt like she could do anything. He had helped make her strong their whole life. Parts of a whole.

"Let's fish before it gets too late to feed our families." She said while blushing and holding his hand.

"I love watching you blush. It let's me know I'm doing a good job." He chuckled.

"Don't forget, I can worm a hook and take most fish off, but if I get a catfish… It's your job."

They fished for about about three hours. In that short amount of time, they caught ten that they had to let go. They weren't completely unsuccessful. They got to keep twenty good sized ones. Shawn went to the truck and grabbed his folding table. They had planned on cleaning the fish at the pond. It fed the animals on the land and kept the mess out of their houses. A sincerely a gross job but someone had to do it, and they picked the right place, all things considered,

It started to sprinkle just as they finished loading the truck up.

"We couldn't have picked a better cut off time if we tried. By the time we get home it'll be time to start dinner. Why don't you go home, shower and grab your dad? We can all eat together." Mellie said.

"That's perfect. He's been wanting to come say hi." Shawn replied. When they pulled up to Mellie's she hopped out and grabbed the cooler of fish.

"Alright babe, I'll just hop in the shower and Dad will probably have half of our catch frying when you two get here. Can't wait to see you in a bit." She waved as Shawn drove off. As she walked into the house it started to downpour. She took a fast shower. As she walked back downstairs her dad and grandpa were running in.

"Whew, everything is all locked up and all the animals are in their barns."

"That's great Dad! We have fish for you to cook up. Can we fry the catfish, and broil the rest?"

"Absolutely bumblebee!"

"Not sure when Shawn will be back, but he's bringing Chuck with him." Mellie said.

"Oh good. We miss having him around." Dad replied.

When Shawn and Chuck walked through the door it was pure magic. Everyone was working on their own special thing for dinner. Dad was frying the catfish, Grandpa was getting ready to broil the other fish, Grandma was making fresh squeezed lemonade, mom was working on dessert, and Mellie was setting the table.

"Everything looks amazing!! And smells even better!" Chuck exclaimed.

"Have a seat and I'll grab you a glass of water." Mellie pulled out a chair. She went to the sink and filled a glass pitcher of water from the spout. They were lucky to not have to deal with well water. She went to the table and poured a glass for Chuck. She then walked to where Shawn was setting, leaned down and pressed her lips to his cheek. She then poured him a glass of water.

"What a lovely host you make." Chuck said with a silly grin as he watched Shawn and Mel.

She giggled and said, "thank you, Chuck. We're all glad to see you."

When dinner was ready everyone sat down. They began to pass the food around. Fried catfish, broiled trout, green beans, hush puppies and fresh squeezed lemonade. They had brownies al a mode for dessert. They ate until they felt like they were bursting at the seams and talked about everything and anything.

"It's been so nice to sit here and get to see the love birds finally together." Chuck said. "Do you know how long he's had a thing for you Mellie?"

"No, please enlighten me!"

"Well, as long as I can remember him talking about girls. You've been the only one on his radar that I ever heard about." The whole thing was overwhelming, but she was so happy to hear it. She knew how he felt about her now, but honestly thought it was something that had developed just those few short weeks ago when she had transformed.

"You sure do know how to make a girl feel special. Now I know where Shawn got it from." He was so red faced he couldn't even attempt to cover it up. It meant so much to him that she finally knew how long Shawn had had feelings for her.

About an hour after dessert Shawn and Chuck headed home. He pecked her on the lips as they walked out. "I'll call you when we get home and settled. Have a good night beautiful."

When she knew the car was down the driveway she began to lightly cry. They were some of the happiest tears she'd ever cried. It was so good knowing that she was desired and cared about before this trip home. She had loved him since their freshman year of high school. She always thought she wouldn't have a chance with someone like him. As she walked upstairs, she called out to her parents and grands, "Goodnight, I love you all so much. Sleep well and see you in the morning."

When she got to her room she changed into some pj's and curled up in her bed with her new book. She had just began to read when her phone rang.

"Hey stranger, I had an amazing time at dinner tonight." said Shawn.

"It was the best time. Especially when your dad told me your little secret." She said with a dimple filled smile.

"I wish he wouldn't have said anything. I was a little embarrassed in front of everyone."

"Shawn, honestly? I don't want you ever to feel embarrassed when it has to do with me. I don't think you understand how much I needed to know what he said." Man was she glad he couldn't see her right now. Dumb smile, red cheeks that hurt from smiling so much, and her makeup running down her face from the happiest adult tears she'd ever had. "I wish you would have told me a lot sooner. I feel like we've missed out on time together."

"We've got forever. I was so sure you didn't like me back and I didn't want that sting of rejection." Shawn honestly said.

"Are you serious?! I've liked you forever. I just didn't think I had a chance with someone like you. Completely put together, gorgeous and so handsome and fit." Mellie couldn't believe she was being this vulnerable. "I never thought I was good enough for someone like you, so I taught myself to be ok with our relationship the way it was."

"I wish I was there right now to show you how wrong you are. You're everything I want and need and more."

"You are too sweet for your own good! We need to sleep. Two more long days of work ahead of us before we set out on our big camping trip." Mellie sighed.

"You're right. I have so much to do. I have to make sure I write a detailed list so Dad doesn't forget to tell my cousin Lenny how everything should be done."

"Oh, no…. Lenny again!?"

"See, now you know the expanse of the details I have to put into this note. Who do you have coming to your farm?"

"Kristine, and Justin from the tack shop. They do such a good job now that they're older. Their parents will come and keep an eye on them the first week then they'll be on their own. Do you want me to have them check on Chuck and Lenny a couple times a week?"

"Babe! That would be amazing! To tell you the truth I was getting so nervous. Dad can still do most of the work, but he needs help. Alright I'm going to get off here. I will talk to you tomorrow. Good night love and sleep well." Shawn hung up before Mellie could respond. She sent him a text.

Sleep well and I'll be dreaming of you: She put her phone down and rolled over. She grabbed her phone one more time.: *I didn't miss the thing you said right before you hung up. But same!*

CHAPTER ELEVEN

When Mellie woke up, she could hear her mother in the kitchen singing. She grabbed her phone and sent Shawn a small morning text. *Today will be busy and I probably won't have my phone much. Have an amazing day and I'll call you around lunch.*

Mellie happily ran down the stairs and put her phone on the charging port. DING: Just as fast as she put it down, she picked it up. *Hey Beautiful! Have the best day and you may see me at some point. I'll be running around with Lenny. Wish me luck!*

You need it! Mellie put the phone down again, walked over to her mom and gave her a big hug.

"Good morning Mom! Are the guys outside already?" Mellie asked while pouring herself a big cup of coffee.

"Yep! Kristine and Justin are here to get the daily routine down. You should run out and say hi. They've been out there for a couple hours now. I'm making them some lemonade. Do you mind running it out to them?"

"Sure Mom!" she grabbed cups and the pitcher. "Love you and we'll be in at lunch!"

Mellie ran outside and saw a big group of people over by the barn. As she got closer, she started to laugh. She turned around and ran back into the house. "Mom, I need two more cups. Looks like Lenny and Shawn are outside."

By the time she got out to the barn they had all sat down. Bandanas were out cleaning sweat and dirt off their faces. She sat the pitcher on the table, walked over to Shawn leaned up and kissed his cheek. Of course, he had to lean down so they would even meet. Lenny looked shocked and confused.

"Excuse me… But when did this happen?" Lenny questioned.

"In my mind, always, but realistically… almost a month." Shawn said blushing.

"It's about time!" Lenny sang.

When they had all been thoroughly hydrated, they finished showing Justin and Kristine the ropes at the farm. Mellie quickly kissed Shawn goodbye and the kids headed over to his farm. They honestly wouldn't be needed. Lenny always did a good job. His issue was that he wanted everything perfect and that wasn't possible on a farm. Before Shawn got too far away Mellie's mom ran out the door.

"Hey, why don't you all head over here for lunch after you get settled there. Bring your dad! We have to empty our fridge before we're gone for a month."

"Absolutely!" Lenny yelled. Shawn punched his arm.

"Dad would love that! An hour enough time?" Shawn asked

"Of course, Honey. I've been cooking all morning it should be ready by then."

Mellie went into the house and grabbed as many duffle bags as she could get her hands on. Packing for a month never took as much time as they thought it would, but it was always better to overpack than under.

"Hey Mom. I'm going to start by packing things for everyone. Towels and things like that. Then I'll start on clothes. Can you let everyone know to leave what they want packed on their beds? I'll start clothes after lunch."

"Sure thing sweety. As long as you remind Shawn that we leave the day after tomorrow."

"I can't believe I've already been here a month. So much has changed. SHIT!!!! I have to make sure I get the edits in before I go to bed tonight."

"Language! Do you have a lot to do?"

"No, I just lost track of time. I may be good for nothing tomorrow. Well, today after lunch honestly. I am a bit behind." Mellie sighed.

No sooner had Mellie started packing than everyone walked in the door. Grandma was just starting to set the table. Dad and Kristine ran over to help her while Justin and Shawn went into the kitchen to help her mom bring stuff to the table. Mellie was carrying a stack of towels she couldn't see over when she bumped into someone.

"Shit I'm sorry!" She yelled.

"No worries. Just walked over to help you." Mellie knew that voice without even trying.

"Thanks Lenny." She said flatly. It's not that she didn't like him, it's just that he had always given her the creeps. Ogling her when they were alone. Always trying to find ways to touch her. "I've got it. Go take a seat. I'll be there shortly."

Lenny huffed and walked away. He sat at the table next to Shawn.

"Hey, Lenny. Scoot over so Mellie can sit by me please." Shawn said.

"Oh hey, of course Cuz." He rolled his eyes as he scooted over a seat. Shawn saw what was happening and moved to the seat in the middle.   "Hey, Mel. I put you between me and Dad. I hope that's ok."

"That's great! I'd love to sit there. I need to know the gossip I don't know on you!" She said with a laugh. When she put the towels down, she walked over and found her seat. She leaned over and kissed Chuck on the cheek then found her way to Shawn with a quick peck on the lips. Shawn saw that something wasn't right. He looked to Lenny and then back at Mellie. He took her hand in his and raised it to his lips. Leaned over and whispered in her ear.

"You'll always be safe with me." He saw the smile creep back to her face and he gently let her hand go.

For the remainder of the meal, they chatted about the trip. They only had a day and a half to get ready. They talked about the caves they had rented to stay in. The list said cabin, but it included Wi-Fi, plumbing and electricity. It was like a fancy hotel built into a hillside cave system. Every room was its own cave. You could pick the amenities you wanted. They had picked the most bougie ones. It had been that way the past couple of years. Her parents and grandparents weren't as young as they once were. They needed the beds and warm baths just to walk most days.

When lunch was done everyone quickly left and Shawn gave a final kiss to Mellie.

"Little birdie told me not to bother you tonight. You have been a bit behind on work. Get caught up. If you need a break just text and we can have a short phone call. I will leave you be so you can get to work. Don't pack until tomorrow. That way you don't have to rush doing it all alone." Shawn said and planted a big kiss on her cheek.

"I'll get to work right now. I will text you later. We'll talk later tonight. I'll make it a priority. Because you are a part of me now. Not talking to you would be like not breathing." Mellie said as she gently kissed his lips.

"Then I'll be awaiting your call."

After everyone had left her mom poured what looked like a gallon of coffee into a thermos and handed it to Mellie.

"Thanks Mom. I will definitely be needing this!"

"All right dear, now get to work."

Mellie walked up the stairs and headed straight to her desk. She checked the last email from her boss. Attached were the four articles she needed to edit and format before she left on her vacation. She opened every article at once and read the first couple paragraphs. These articles were all written pretty well and they shouldn't take her too long. An hour later she had sent the first article back. She quickly started article two. She thought this would be a fast one as well. She was mistaken. It took her two hours and the entire thermos of coffee. She reached for her cup and pushed send on that article. Editing that one was like watching paint dry. Boring and tedious.

She hit the bottom of the stairs at the perfect time. Her mom met her with a plate of food and an entire pitcher of sweet tea.

"It's not that I don't want to see you, but you have work to do."

"Yes ma'am. Thanks a ton Mom. I have two more articles to do. I'll bring down my plate when I'm finished."

"I'll come get it after we're done eating."

"Thanks again Mom." She took her food to her desk and opened her next article. This one was about how to find true love. It was the worst article ever written. Such a load of garbage. She had always felt this way about these kind of articles. At first it was because she had never experienced love. At least not true love. Now it was worse because the advice was just bad. However, that was not her job. She'd format and edit and then her boss would make the final decision.

2 ½ hours later she was still editing this terrible piece of "journalism". She decided to take a break just as the door opened.

"Mom, this is the worst thing I've ever read. It's a bunch of garbage about what a woman needs to do to find the perfect man. All the things she needs to change. I HATE IT!!!"

"Oh, sweet girl. Why don't you just finish this really quick, and then take a small break?"

"That's the plan. I love you and I'll see you in the morning. Please don't wake me up. I'll miss breakfast if my body deems it so."

"Ok baby. Goodnight. I'll leave you be."

With more determination than she'd ever needed before she finished the article an hour later. It had never taken Mellie this long to finish something before. Either it was that bad or she was losing her touch. She sent it in and opened the fourth and final article. This one was sure to be interesting.

She wasn't wrong. She had never had the opportunity to edit one of the stories in the back of the magazine. It was pure smut and she blushed the entire time she worked on it. 45 minutes later she was done and sent it in. With a huge sigh she lay back on her bed and picked her phone up. Shawn had really done it. All day and not one distraction. She called him and he picked up on the first ring.

"I was starting to think you didn't want to talk to me." Shawn joked.

"Don't be silly! I always want to talk to you. I just finished. In order I edited them: <u>The Great Melt</u>-we've got a guy that writes about the planet every month. It's always easy to edit and easier to read.

*<u>10 Ways to Cook Egg Plant</u>- yuck… The woman we have on our health and wellness page. Everything she says is great but she's not a very good writer, so it took me forever.

<u>Find the Man of Your Dreams</u>- ugh… It was awful! This woman who has been married since she was 18 and a day always writes these crazy articles about what we as woman need to do to impress men.

<u>Holy SMUT</u>… OMG I've never had the pleasure of editing any of these stories and I couldn't stop blushing the whole time.

They are all done and sent it. I just laid down and I missed your voice.

So, how was the rest of your day?"

"Really good. Lenny and I got his room all set up. I'm telling him not to go to your place while you're gone. I've also talked to Kristine's mom and dad. They are going to help over here so the kids don't get over worked."

"Aww babe. That's so sweet and thoughtful. I'm also glad that Lenny won't be anywhere near Kristine. She's to young for his advances."

"That's the real reason. I want everyone to have a safe and fun month when we're away. They're all staying at your place, right?"

"Eric and the kids are. Shelly is going to be running back and forth to their tack store."

"That's great! So, are you ready for this trip? I can't wait to be in nature with you for a month. Nature adjacent." He chuckled.

"It'll be great. I got us a cave that's a little more rugged but not completely." Mellie laughed. "Alright, I have to lay down. I've got an unbelievable headache from those awful articles, but at least they're finished."

"Alright. Goodnight and I will be dreaming of you." Shawn said

"I always dream of you and that won't change tonight." Mellie said as she drifted off to sleep.

CHAPTER TWELVE

When Mellie woke up and rolled over. She looked at her phone and sat up with a start. 'OMG' she thought. She had never fallen asleep on the phone before, but apparently, last night had changed all that. The most nerve racking part was that he hadn't hung up either.

"Oh, shit!" she yelled.

"Good morning." she heard a groggy Shawn say on the other end of the phone.

"Oh my God… I can't believe you listened to me fall asleep. Snoring, I'm sure. How embarrassing! Oh, good morning right back at you." She said shyly.

"Babe, you actually didn't snore. You do, however, make the cutest noises ever when you're falling asleep. Don't worry, I fell asleep not long after you. My phone is absolutely dead now though, so I'll talk to you later." Shawn said right before he hung up.

Mellie rolled out of bed and walked downstairs. She had expected everyone to be outside working already but they had just sat down at the table for what looked like a massive breakfast.

"Good morning honey." Amelia said as she handed her a cup of coffee. "You're up early."

"Well, all things considered I fell asleep rather early. Woke up to the realization that Shawn and I fell asleep on the phone together so now I'm dying of embarrassment."

"He didn't mind one bit did he Love?" Aileen questioned.

"No Mom, he thought I made cute noises as I fell asleep." She blushed.

"I knew he was a keeper." Callum chuckled.

Mellie sat down next to her dad and hugged him.

"I think so too." She said with a smile.

"So, what's on the agenda for today for everyone?" Mom asked as she piled food on everyone's plates.

There was no getting around huge portions while they were trying to eat up a nice chunk of their food before they left for their camping trip.

"I have to pack. That will take me a large part of the day, I'm sure.

Remind me when it's time for lunch or I will surely forget."

"Sure, thing Dear. I am going to be making the beds for our guests and running to the store for some staples. The Stevens will be bringing most of their own food as they eat much differently than us. I'd still like to go grab some milk and eggs to get them started." Mom said, and Grandma nodded.

"We'll be stocking up on animal feed and making sure everyone is taken care of and where they need to be. We'll probably be running the perimeter and checking the fences to make sure everything is holding up."

"Whew!" Mellie exclaimed. "It's sure going to be a busy day for all of us. I probably won't get the chance to see Shawn until dinner." Mom had invited everyone over to talk about the trip a bit more. They were to leave first thing in the morning.

The packing happened faster than she thought it would, she even had time to help her grandparents. At that point Mellie decided to go check on everyone else. Callum and Angus were at the fences as they walked the perimeter of the farm. The newer fences had been holding up nicely. Mellie checked all the cameras. The technology often drove them nuts, but it would be so helpful to make sure nothing was happening, and if it did, they would see it immediately. Angus had made sure to give the family that would be staying at the farm all they needed to access the cameras. Mellie had talked to them about not letting Lenny get close to Kristine. He'd hit on her once and was extremely inappropriate. With a young girl on the farm, she wanted to make sure that all their bases were covered.

They skipped lunch that day as they were planning on a late afternoon dinner to get to bed around 8 so they could head out as early as possible. Aileen had made a significantly smaller meal which was good because they had been getting so stuffed Mellie knew she couldn't do it again. She decided to help set the table and make a wonderful hibiscus iced tea to go with their meal. Aileen and decided on a cream based pasta dish, a wonderful caesar salad and some homemade garlic bread would hit the spot after everyone's long day. Amelia had worked painstakingly on a huge peach cobbler and would be served with homemade whipped cream and vanilla ice cream. They knew they wouldn't get meals like this for the next two months, so they decided to overindulge.

They got the table set just in time. The Stevens, Shawn, Chuck and Lenny all walked in at the perfect time. Mellie had put in all three table extenders and brought in all the extra chairs they could manage to fit around the table. She had to stop herself from making a seating chart to make sure Lenny was far away from her and Kristine. It was easier than she expected. Lenny sat down between Shawn and his dad, Mellie sat next to Shawn and the Stevens sat next to her. They sat and ate until no one could stuff anymore into their mouths. Then they got to talking.

"So, Angus, when do you suppose we'll head out tomorrow?" Shawn asked.

"You and Mellie can head out whenever you wish. We'll be leaving around 4:30am." Angus answered.

"That's about the time I was thinking." Mellie interjected. "It'll give us enough time to get everything unloaded and set up in the caves. Leaving us enough time to find that waterfall we all love so much and take a dip."

"There's a little place I'd love to take you at some point tomorrow." Shawn said rubbing his hand on her thigh.

"I'd love to see what you have to show me." Mellie blushed. She heard a grumble from a couple seats away. She knew who it was and what his problem was. His jealousy was unreal and unwarranted.

"Mellie, Shawn, Grandpa and I would like to train with you at least one hour twice a day. I hope that doesn't thwart your plans." Dad said.

"Straight to business as always Dad!" Mellie joked. "I was figuring it would be something like that."

"Training for what?" Lenny questioned.

"Just building muscle and stamina. It's something we do on these trips every year. This is, however, the first year Mellie will join us." Her dad answered but said no more.

Just then Aileen and Amelia brought dessert to the table. They figured everyone had had enough time to make a little room.

Mellie scooped cobbler onto everyone's plate. Aileen brought around the ice cream and Amelia dolloped whipped cream on top. It looked and smelled amazing. They pretty much ate in silence. It was early but all the work that day had worn them out. When dessert was over everyone got ready to leave.

"Alright," Said Eric, "we'll be back with our stuff tomorrow morning. Shelly will be primarily running the store, so it'll be the three of us. Kristine and Chad are so excited to help and quite frankly so am I. It's nice to move away from the norm sometimes."

"We're so happy you'll be helping. We'd trust no one else with our livelihood." Mom said giving them all hugs.

"Yes! 1,000 thank you's!" Mellie exclaimed.

"We're headed off to bed. Thank you so much for helping and for becoming part of our family!" Amelia said hugging them all as well.

"Alright Love we're headed out. I'll be here around 4:00am tomorrow so we can load the last bit into my truck." Shawn said. He wrapped his arms around Mellie's waist and pulled her in for a quick yet passionate kiss.

Lenny slammed the door as he walked outside. It actually made Mellie and Shawn chuckle.

When everyone had left the family said their goodnights and headed to bed. When Mellie got to her room, she grabbed her phone and sent a quick text to Shawn.

I can't wait to spend the next two months sleeping next to you! Where are you taking me tomorrow?

That's a secret. Babe, I've never asked anything of you like this, but do you think tomorrow you can wear a dress and maybe no panties?

Mellie blushed so brightly when she saw this message that she snapped a picture and sent it to him.

Yes, my only guess as to why is very exciting I can't wait to feel your hands on my body again. It's been far too long.

Good night my love. I'll see you bright and early

CHAPTER THIRTEEN

The alarm went off way too early in Mellie's honest opinion. 3:30am is never fun for anyone but especially for a woman whose whole life was literally about to change. She was ready, but for what she wasn't exactly sure. She grabbed some things to do in the car as she was going to be a total passenger princess.

She threw on her favorite skirt and tank top. Comfort was key. She walked down the stairs and to no ones surprise she was the last one to arrive. She walked around and gave out hugs. When she reached Shawn, he grabbed her right hand and spun her around while whistling. She had never felt so beautiful. She wrapped her arms around his neck, and he bent down and gently kissed her on the lips. They all poured coffee down their throats and headed to their cars. Their trip was only a bit over 2 ½ hours but getting there early was their goal. They'd have the whole day to get situated. They hopped into their cars and hit the road.

"Hey beautiful, are you excited about this trip?" Shawn asked while placing his right hand on her thigh.
"More than you know. You and I will finally have some much needed time to ourselves. I get to start my training, whatever that entails and I just can't wait to be one with nature." It would be an amazing day!

The ride was nice and calm. Roads were clear as they had left so early. They didn't even stop to use the restroom. It was quite perfect. When they got to the park they had to wait about twenty minutes for the rest of the family to show up.

"Mom and Grandma probably had them stop two times at least so they could use the bathroom." Mellie laughed.

"You know, those old bladders!" Shawn chuckled back.

When the rest of the family pulled in to their spots the party really started. "Party" being another bathroom stop on their way to check into their caves. About twenty minutes later they found their way into their three neighboring hotel rooms.

"Alright, I love you all." Sighed Grandma. "However, I am going to take a much-needed nap and unpack. I will see you for dinner."

"Same," said Callum, "some wonderful cool cave air will be amazing on these old knees."

"Sounds about the same for us." agreed Shawn. "Then I'm going to take Mellie somewhere special."

CHAPTER FOURTEEN

They entered their room, dropped their bags and collapsed on the bed.

"3:30am is way too early." Mellie said as she slid next to Shawn. She curled up in his big strong arms and woke up three hours later. They began their adventure around 11:00am. Mellie changed into a summer dress that was mid thigh and a comfy pair of hiking sandals. Surprisngly, Mellie had found that they did exist. Under it she wore her bathing suit. You know, just in case Shawn decided on another surprise swim. They headed out for what Shawn was hoping would be a romantic adventure.

He had planned the whole thing out and even memorized a map of the falls location so he was sure not to get lost. He was scared. Today was the day he was going to tell her a secret she needed to know before training started. He wasn't sure how she'd react and that was terrifying. Shawn was hoping it would be a good thing.

They headed out on their adventure and after about an hour of holding hands and taking photos of the amazing summer flowers and wildlife they could hear their destination in the distance. Sure enough, through the next clearing of trees they arrived at the clearest and most beautiful fresh water pool they had ever seen. The water fall was a gentle trickle as it hadn't rained much lately, but the pool was deep. They took off their shoes and let their feet enter the water.

"This is one of the most beautiful things I've ever seen." Mellie said with a sigh.

"It's probably because it's one of the least known falls in the park. Not a lot of foot traffic so there's been no damage." Shawn said while ringing his hands from nerves.

"Babe, what's going on? You seem a bit off today. Nervous about something if I'm being honest." Mellie asked.

"I am nervous. I've been meaning to tell you something and I'm not sure how you're going to react. I need to tell you before we start training and since that's tomorrow, I can't hold out any longer."

"Well, now I'm nervous… I can't tell you how I'll react because I don't know what it is. I can tell you I love you and I may need time, but you've got me, and I've got you."

"Did you just say you love me? I love you to, and I can't wait to see what the future holds." Shawn said as he turned towards Mellie and held both her hands.

"Ok, so first things first. I know what you are. Or at least I know as much as your dad and grandpa know. As much as you know. They told me when we started dating so that I wouldn't be shocked and so it would be easier to tell you what i am about to say." Shawn said while rubbing circles on the back of Mellie's palms.

"I figured you knew. I am not upset about that at all. Especially since you are bound to see that within the next month. I am kind of bummed I didn't get to tell you. It does explain why they assured me that you would be ok with the news. Those old goats! They've got an earful coming." Mellie laughed.

"Don't be too hard on them. They just wanted to make sure I was prepared. For what? I'm not sure. "Shawn said with a laugh. "Ok, now on to the thing you don't know. Your family already knows, and they have for years. I wasn't sure I'd ever be confident enough to tell you but here goes. I am a shifter as well." he said while not making eye contact.

"What!? I didn't know that any others existed. I had no clue. Just you or are there others?" Mellie questioned as she squeezed his hands.

"From what I've been told there are many. The genes tend to run in families. My father, his father, that type of thing. I am a wolf shifter too. I don't change like your family does though. Strictly full moons like in the movies."

"First let me say I'm not mad. But I am confused. There's just so much I don't know. I'm glad you told me. Not sure how I would have reacted if I just saw you change with no warning. Does it hurt?"

"It doesn't feel great. At least not the first couple of times. You get used to it, but it takes a bit to get over the fact that you're an animal all of the sudden. Do you think you're ready?" Shawn asked.

"Ummm… Yes? But also, hell no. Scared as hell, because a female shifter is almost unheard of. At least in the recent past. I don't know what's going to happen. Here I go rambling… It's the nerves." Mellie said almost shaking.

They had planned to swim and enjoy the sunset, but as they sat and talked for hours the evening chill started. They decided to go back to camp, check on the 'rents and grandparents, let everyone know that they had no more secrets and start a fire. The walk back was a bit faster. It was going to storm. The temperature had dropped significantly. Even for an

Ohio summer evening. When they got back to the caves the parents had already started a fire and dinner. They were excited because they hadn't even thought of food on their adventure. They walked up and got a seat around the fire.

"How was your adventure?" Dad asked, with a knowing look.

"First of all, YOU SUCK but also thank you for preparing him. It went really well." Mellie said laughing.

"To be fair," Shawn said, "It was a little obvious pretty immediately. Your whole body had changed."

"I know..." Mellie said. "You have no idea the shock that went through my body when I woke up hugely muscled with a freaking unibrow! I still have to shave my eyebrows everyday. I wake up being a hairy dog every. Single. Day..."

They began to eat and chit-chat throughout the early evening and well into the night. When the fire had burned out, they all went to their rooms. Training did start tomorrow, and it would be the full moon... Mellie and Shawn walked into their room and began to get ready for bed. Mellie had just began to disrobe when she felt Shawn at her back. He gently wrapped his arms around her waist.

"You know, I loved you before the change. I was just so timid to say anything. I was also scared that you wouldn't react well to my wolf side." "Now look at us. Both shifters, I'm a freaking huge beast, and tomorrow I try with my first shift." Mellie said nervously.

"I know Babe. You'll be great. I just know it." Shawn said while wrapping her in his arms. "You know tonight probably wouldn't be a good time to get frisky, but I would love to cuddle you all night long just as you are."

"Are you asking for us to sleep naked?" She teased.

"Well, yes, I am. It'll keep us from getting overheated which happens before a full moon. It'll also be easy to keep cooler because we'll be sleeping so close together. The best of both worlds if you ask me."

They got undressed and curled up together in bed. They were asleep before they knew what hit them.

CHAPTER FIFTEEN

Mellie woke up in a sweat. She had had the recurring nightmare. It had been a nightly occurrence since the change. She was woken up every night by a woman falling to the ground, being attacked by soldiers and telling them she'd be back. She had no idea why this dream kept happening nor what it meant. It made her sick to her stomach some days. The things these men did to her were unforgivable.

She rolled over and looked at her phone. 4:00am…. This was no good. She'd need more sleep in order to be able to function today. She rolled back over, tucked her head into the crook of Shawn's arm and drifted back to sleep. When she woke up four hours later it was to her being poked in her lower back. This was the first time they had spent a full night together and she had forgotten morning excitement was even a thing.

Shawn wrapped his arms around her and pulled her closer still. He let out a low moan. It let Mellie realize he liked the way that she felt but also let her know that he was still fast asleep. She slowly began to roll her hips against his ever growing pleasure spot. With her hand she began to trail her fingers over his arms lightly. Mellie brought his arm up to her mouth and gently kissed it. Still rotating her hips, she laid his hand to rest on her excited nipples. He moaned and she knew he had woken up fully when his other hand found a sensitive spot right on the side of her neck. She moaned as he gently pinched her nipple.

"Good morning Handsome. How'd you sleep?"

"Wonderful. I can't think of sleeping anymore. Lay on your back for me Princess." Mellie rolled onto her back and let her hand trail down to Shawn's thigh. His hands roamed her lower stomach and found their way to his favorite spot. He began to circle her growing bud. Her moans had become music to his ears. She tried to get up onto her knees. She loved pleasing him with her mouth, but he pushed her back down. "Not today. You are mine this morning and I want the world to know that you feel pleasure like no one I've ever seen or heard."

"Yes please. However, don't forget that most of these people are my family."

"Trust me, during the change it's expected and if I don't start to make you scream soon, you'll hear them doing it, and I know neither of us wants that." Shawn said as he laid down in between her legs.

"Please hurry! I can't hear that. It'll ruin my life." She giggled before she let out a long moan caused by Shawn's tongue running the length of her slit. He then started to concentrate on her clit as his fingers found their way inside her. It didn't take long for him to bring her to her first of two orgasms. She had never felt this powerful or this much longing before. She didn't know what over took her but before she knew what happened she had rolled Shawn onto his back and straddled him. She wasn't gentle and by the look in his eyes he was happy about that. She lowered herself onto him with a speed and power that she had never used before and she saw Shawn's eyes roll into the back of his head. He let out a long strong growl and a moan as she began to ride him hard. Shawn placed his hands on her hips and made every thrust stronger and deeper.

"Babe, if you don't quit," Mellie said," I'm going to cum again."

"That's the point love. Now fuck me like you've never done before." Shawn said. She continued at the same pace but with more strength and added a rotation in her hips. She came two more times back to back.

Before she knew what was happening Shawn picked her up, put her on her knees and was behind her entering her from the back. He shoved her face into the bed and held onto her shoulders as he pounded her until she climaxed too many more times to count.

"Oh My God babe! Please don't stop." Mellie screamed.

"Never my dear girl. This pussy, and ass are mine today!"

She had never felt this way before but she needed him to fill every hole. She felt like an animal and she knew he did too. He continued to pound her from the back until she was screaming yet again. He pulled out of her. His cock was covered in her juices and as she moaned she felt him begin to press into her ass. She hadn't done it often, but she did enjoy it. It must be part of the change, but she opened up easily and before she knew it, she was coming again. Shawn started to increase his speed and force. She knew he was close, so she started to thrust backwards to meet him every time. Before she felt him empty inside of her, she came again with a growl she had never let out before.

"Oh, there she is." Shawn purred in her ear. At only those words she lost control again.

"OH MY GOD! I could do this all day." Mellie sighed and lay back on the bed.

"Oh, my love. We will many more times today and more tonight. We will eat and train in between, but this is pretty standard for the change nights."

"I may like this more than I already did." Mellie laughed.

"Oh, Babe me too. I have never had a partner during a change. I was always too afraid. I stuck to my hands but this my dear, is so. Much. Better."

As they went into the bathroom she looked in the mirror.

"FUCK!!! What the hell is this?!" Mellie's unibrow was back with a vengeance and her eyes had turned pale blue with little black pupils.

"Look at me Mellie. You're beautiful and you're in the middle of change day. You'll look like this every day of the change. It's normal. However, I've never seen eyes like that." Shawn said as he gently kissed her forehead and cheek. "Let's shower and go eat. Sounds safe enough to go check on everyone else." They both laughed.

After their shower, which included a couple more handmade orgasms they were dressed and sitting around the picnic table. Her parent's and grandparent's were sitting on the other side of the table just staring at her.

"Your eyes." Her dad said. "We've never seen anything like it. We've heard but never seen. There are stories about the Eternal Lady and her eyes of ice blue. But that can't be. Can it Dad?"

"Son, I don't know. This is all so new to us. She looks like the stories, but what does this mean about the change?"

"Why, what is going to happen?" Mellie worried.

"I'm sure it's nothing dear." Her mother reassured her.

They ate a hearty meal. After they tore all the food up, they made excuses to go back to their rooms for 'naps'. Mellie wasn't dumb and she wasn't surprised as Shawn and she hadn't been able to stop rubbing their hands all over each other during the meal. It went on like this the entire day.

Running with the shifters, eating, orgasms, hand-to-hand combat, and other super physical activities. All day, but not in that order. All day, and no exhaustion Mellie had energy like she'd never had before. As the sun went down instead of getting tired Mellie got more energized. She thought she could go for another two days on this energy alone.

CHAPTER SIXTEEN

The shifters talked in detail about where they would be for the change. They couldn't be around Mom and Grandma. They had never been put their wives in danger. However, with this being Mellie's first change and without any knowledge of how that would look they decided to play it safe. They decided on a beautiful nature filled spot where they could be as loud as they needed to be. They started their run around 6:30pm after dinner. They soon found themselves in a clearing. There were tall trees in every direction, wonderful flowers everywhere. It was like all of Mellie's senses were heightened. She could hear everything. Even the grass blowing in the breeze. She heard what she was sure was her mom and grandma singing together, but she didn't know how. They were so far away.

As the sun continued to go down, they all started to get jittery. Mellie had it worst of all. It was like her skin was itching. She couldn't get comfortable. Nothing specifically hurt but everything just felt yuck. Shawn was rolling around in the grass and it made Mellie chuckle.

"Shawn! You've never looked cuter in your life." Mellie joked.

"Leave me alone! It's the only thing that makes the everything stop!" he laughed.

"If that's the case." Mellie lay down on the ground and started rolling around. She didn't know why or how, but she instantly felt better. Dad and Grandpa both started laughing and rolling their eyes. They were just sitting there on logs smoking their pipes.

"Why doesn't this happen to you?" Mellie asked.

"Well, we're old and have been at this a long time. It stops being so uncomfortable after a while." Dad said.

"Can't wait for that day. So, I'll just roll around until I change I guess." Mellie said.

"That's what Shawn does every time, and we still laugh at him." Grandpa laughed.

"They're not lying. I don't know why I still do this with those grumpy old men." Shawn joked.

Without any knowledge of what was happening Mellie saw it before she felt it. She looked around her and all the men were growing huge and hairy. Well, hairier than normal. Before her very eyes she saw three wolves she'd ever seen. She could tell who was who instantly. Her dad and grandpa were salt and pepper gray and way bigger than Shawn. She knew that was because they became humanoid wolves for their major change. Shawn was gorgeous. Black and shiny with the most beautiful green eyes she'd ever seen.

She didn't get to enjoy the sight for long though. All of the sudden it felt like she was bending in half. It didn't hurt per se. It just felt so strange. The other wolves were looking at her with what could only be described as curiosity, and she didn't know why. That was until she became bigger than them. the woods and saw a long white tail behind her, and hooves. Mellie found the clo She ran throughsest body of water and looked into like a mirror. She had become a horse. The most magnificent white horse she'd ever ever seen. She was huge, and beautiful. She ran back into the clearing and the wolves began to howl. She was scared but only for a moment. They surrounded her and started to sniff. She knew she was safe.

Then in her head she heard.

"Run little horse. Pretend we're chasing you to hurt you." It had to be her dad, but she wasn't sure. She was hearing thoughts and that was scary.

"Do it little one." her grandpa said.

She started to run. They were chasing her, but she wasn't scared. She didn't know why they wanted this, but she kept running. The wolves were faster than her and she didn't know what to do.

"Change!" her dad yelled as he ran past.

She didn't know what he meant exactly but tried to think of running faster than them. She felt like she could run faster than them, so she did her best, and as she had expected she soon caught up and passed them all. She had just passed them when she felt a nip on the back of her leg. She let out a growl and instantly was a large white wolf. They all howled.

"I'm sorry kid. I just needed to see if it was true." her dad said in her head.

"See if what was true Dad?"

"You're her. Well, a new 'her'. You're the Eternal Lady. You can be and shift into whatever you need to be."

CHAPTER SEVENTEEN

She was so confused. As they ran around that evening, mostly in the clearing, she just laid curled in a little ball. Like a puppy whimpering in fear. They kept trying to get Mellie to play but she just didn't know what to think. A month ago, she was just a normal, mostly invisible woman. Bigger than average, quiet and quite a good writer. Now, she was… Well, she didn't know what she was, or what it meant. It seemed overwhelming already.

When 2:00am rolled around the guys had worn themselves out.

Callum and Angus had run after a couple regular wolves for a reason unknown to Mellie and Shawn found his way to her. She hadn't moved much since her double change. He didn't say anything to her he just wrapped his dark fur covered body around hers. She laid her head on him and began to cry.

"What's wrong Love? I know this is new, but you did great and you're stunning." Shawn thought to her while licking the back of her neck. She sighed gently.

"I'm scared. No one knows anything about who or what I am. No one has a clue as to what I'm going to do or change into. This is all just a cluster fuck. For some reason I was the one chosen to go through this. So much for a quiet life." Mellie let all the emotions out.

Shawn gently ran a paw down her fur. She let out a low sensual growl. Shawn nuzzled her on the top of the head gently.

"Not tonight Mel. You're emotionally raw. Let's get frisky in the morning, for now we just need each other's closeness." Shawn said gently.

"Can you be the sweetest man and wolf in the world? Yes, you can. I am so sexually frustrated, but I know all I need is to be wrapped in your warmth." Mellie said and without another word they both dozed off into a wonderful sleep.

When Mellie woke up, she was herself again. The birds were chirping, and she was still wrapped in Shawn's arms. Shawn's big muscular naked arms. She heard noise coming through the trees and started to freak out a bit.

"BABE!!! Someone's coming! Wake up now, we need to get dressed!"

"Mel, it's most likely Callum and Angus." He sighed and rolled over.

"ALL THE MORE REASON TO GET UP!!! They can't see me naked!" Shawn laughed and got up. They got dressed quickly. Just as Callum and Angus walked through the clearing. They walked up to Mellie and wrapped her in their arms, with tears of joy and pride in their eyes.

"We can get weepy later… Put some damn clothes on!!!"

"Sorry Mellie" Callum said. "We're just so used to being naked and we knew you needed a hug after last night."

After Callum and Angus got dressed they headed back to the caves. They were all so exhausted that they didn't even take time to eat. They just laid down and slept for another four hours. Aileen and Amelia must have been used to this because when they all woke up Mellie smelled the best food she had ever smelled in her whole life. She got up and walked into the bathroom. She stood in front of the mirror and laughed out loud.

"Mel, what's so funny?" Shawn said as he walked into the bathroom.

"Absolutely everything! Look, my unibrow is gone! Today is the first time I haven't had to shave my face since my birthday." Mellie said practically jumping up and down.

"Hurry up and get ready you silly woman. I'm starving and by the smell of it, breakfast is going to be amazing" Shawn said while getting dressed.

CHAPTER EIGHTEEN

Ten minutes later they were all sitting around the picnic tables with their plates piled high. Mellie had never been hungrier in her life. She was so busy gorging herself that at first she didn't even think about what had happened the previous night.

"So…?" Amelia said.

"Oh, Grandma…," Mellie looked up with tears in her eyes. "I didn't change into a wolf. Well, at least not at first. I was a horse. I was a massive white horse. But then Dad bit me on the ankle and before I knew what was happening, I changed into a wolf." Mellie was shaking and Shawn grabbed her hand.

"Callum?" His mother said questioningly.

"We don't know Mom. We have a suspicion. Actually, I'm pretty certain that the stories were all true and that Mellie is the Eternal Lady come back to us. We didn't test it much because it was scary for her, but yeah, that's what we're thinking." Callum sighed.

Mellie sat there just staring into space. Not having anything to say.

She didn't know what to do, or what to say. In reality, last night had been incredible. The horse she had shifted into was unbelievably stunning, and the wolf even more so. It just seemed, however, that she was getting shocks at every turn. Why did her life have to change so drastically at every turn? Shawn just sat beside her with his hand running circles on the small of her back. He had no idea how much it was helping her. He had quickly become her comfort.

"I have an idea." said Shawn. "Would it be possible to maybe go to where your family comes from?"

"Do you mean to the Shetland Islands?" Aileen asked.

"Yes. Here's what I was thinking. If we go there, we can look for more information they may have on the Eternal Lady. Things you may not have access to. Any way to learn anything, really." Shawn continued.

Callum looked at Angus with questions in their eyes.

"I actually think that could be a great idea. I'm just not sure how we'll pull it off with the change. Not the monthly so much, but the ten month." Angus said.

"Why don't we cut this trip a bit short and go on a long distance family trip? Say maybe two weeks here and then head there for two weeks." Amelia asked.

"I don't want to ruin our summer..." sighed Mellie.

"Ruin? Scotland is not going to ruin our summer! Callum has never been and your grandpa and I haven't been in at least fifty years. It will be great! It's the most beautiful place we've ever been. You'll love it." Amelia said.

"If you all are sure it won't ruin our summer. Let's do it. Enjoy two more weeks here training and hiking, then head there. I don't know what we'll be able to find out, but something is better than nothing." Mellie said, still slightly defeated.

Shawn gave Mellie a hug. "The Scottish Highlands with my girl. It couldn't be a better way to end the summer."

They finished eating and went to their respective caves. Mellie flopped down on the huge wooden framed bed and sighed deeply. She was still so lost and confused. She was also very frustrated that she went against her first thought and didn't bring the books about the Wulver history. She thought she knew what and who she was and now everything was changing. She got up and headed into the bathroom. She needed a shower after her long night in fur.

CHAPTER NINETEEN

She slid out of her clothes and decided last minute to hop into the huge jacuzzi tub that had been built into the side wall of the bathroom. Kind of in a cave of its own. She turned the water on and to her surprise it ran out of the wall. It was as if a waterfall filled the tub.

"Shawn! Come look at this!" She yelled with an ounce more excitement than she should have had in these circumstances. Anything to bring her a little joy was welcome at this moment.

"Oh babe. I love what I'm seeing." He said as he wrapped his arms around her from behind.

"Not me silly. The waterfall that's filling up the tub." She hadn't taken her eyes of it.

"Wow, that is beautiful. Why don't you hop in and soak. I have to find a place with cell service so I can call my dad and let him know about the change of plans. Then, if you'll let me, I'd love to slide in behind you in that tub." He said while kissing the nape of her neck.

"Mmmm," She moaned, "I'd love that." Mellie said while pushing her naked ass up against his ever hardening cock.

He kissed her passionately on the mouth and walked out of the bathroom readjusting himself. That made her chuckle.

Mellie climbed into the tub, turned on the jets and closed her eyes. A couple of months ago her life had been normal. She now had no idea who or what she was.

'Ye ken wha yer 'n' ye'll learn more soon enough. I'm so happy to finally have a place to call home after all these years.' Whispered a voice in her head with a deep Scottish accent.

She looked around like she was expecting someone to be standing beside her. That was silly because she knew it came from inside her. Again, she just didn't understand.

"Who are you, and where are you?" Mellie asked.

'A'm Morrigan. Who they call the Eternal Lady. A'm in ye now 'n' ye'v git a' the power and more it seems.' Morrigan said gently.

"Mel, I'm back. Just give me a second and I'll join you." Shawn called from the bedroom.

Mellie jumped like she had been doing something wrong.

"I'm in here waiting." She said sheepishly. "Can you go somewhere during private moments or are you always going to be here?"

Morrigan laughed.

'A'm only 'ere whin yi'll need me, 'n' clearly that isnae noo. Ah will be back dear' and with that the Morrigan was gone.

Just then Shawn strolled into the room wrapped in just a towel. He dropped it to the floor and Mellie's heart skipped a beat. She also felt a heat between her legs.

"Get in here sexy." Mellie said with a purrr.

"As you wish." Shawn slid into the tub behind Mellie and pulled her back so he could hold her.

They lay that way for a while. His arms around her with her head on his furry chest. His legs were out straight on either side of her and her legs were wide open propped up on his legs.

Shawn started to run his hands down her arms and across her collarbones which made Mellie sigh. It's hard to be sure since they were in water, but she had never been this wet. It probably had something to do with the fact that she was so upset last night that in the middle of her first change she couldn't have a sexual release.

"So," Shawn said as he slid his hands down her side. "You seem more relaxed than when I left you to call Dad.

"I am. I'll tell you why. But later. Right now, I need your hands on me, and I don't want to talk about anything other than how good we feel when we touch each other." Mellie said as she repositioned herself so she was sitting on his lap. Still facing away from him but her ass was now on his shaft. She started to rub him up and down just using her ass.

"I'm more than ok with that." Shawn said as he moved his hands up and gently pinched her right nipple between his thumb and forefinger.

"Mmm," she moaned. "Please do it harder."

He did just as he asked. Her back arched and she began to shake as just that one action made her cum with a force she didn't know was possible. Shawn chuckled.

"If this is going to be how you are after every change we may spend our nights as wolves just cuddling. I like this rough side of you." He said as he leaned down and bit the sensitive spot on her neck.

"Holy shit, please do it to the other side!" She pleaded. He did and she came again.

Every time she came, she could feel him getting bigger. It was like her pleasure made him even larger and harder than she had previously felt during their times of intimacy. His left hand gently slid up around her neck and his right hand trailed down to the bud between her legs. He started to run his finger around in circles. Causing every nerve ending in her body to tingle. It didn't take long before she was on the cusp. He felt it building up and adding a bit of pressure to her neck. She yelled out in pleasure and as she came, he removed his hands, lifted her up and entered her. He gently placed her all the way down on his lap again. Every inch of him was inside her. She had never felt anything like this and as he lifted her and then let her slide back down her eyes rolled into the back of her head.

"Holy shit, babe! Please fuck me harder. Please. I don't want nor do I need gentle. I need you to take me!" She begged as she came again.

He was more than willing to oblige. He picked her up and put her on her knees. His cock never left her body. As he positioned himself behind her he gently rocked back and forth just to keep her pleasure building. When they were both in an optimal position, he grabbed her hips on both sides and slid into her so hard and fast the water started to splash out of the tub. He gave it a couple more gently thrusts and didn't go all the way. She had never felt him in this state and he was afraid to go all the way. He didn't want to hurt her.

"Please… More. Give me everything you've got!" Mellie moaned

"Ok. If you're sure."

"More than sure. I need it hard and fast. Choke me. Slap me. Take me." Mellie screamed.

With the consent he needed and wanted, he grabbed her hips on both sides and slammed into her all the way to the hilt. Her orgasm was instant, and she had to grab onto the walls of the cave to keep from collapsing.

By the time they were done she had no idea how many times she had cum. She did know that she couldn't feel her legs, and she was going to need help getting out of the tub. She also knew she wasn't going to move from the bed until, probably, dinner.

Shawn got out of the tub and gently picked up Mellie. He walked her to the bed and laid her down. He grabbed the blanket and covered her. Instead of getting dressed he lay down beside her and kissed her gently on the cheek.

"I love you and I hope you enjoyed that as much as you seemed to."

"I love you too, and yes, I enjoyed it. I can promise you that. You may have to bring me lunch in bed later, because I don't think I'm going to be able to walk until dinner." She laughed.

"Of course, Beautiful." He said and started to run her hands through Mellie's hair.

"Don't start that. I'll need more and I can't right now."

Shawn laughed. "Ok Love, I need to get dressed and go run with the guys anyway."

"Can you please let them know that I'm going to be booking the flight and the stay for our trip? That way we don't have multiple people booking flights." Mellie asked.

"Of course my love, but promise me you'll nap first. You've had a long twenty four hours." Shawn said.

"I promise." She said as she gently closed her eyes.

CHAPTER TWENTY

T he next thing she knew she was being woken up by the smell of, what she assumed was potroast. Shawn had brought her a plate piled with beef, potatoes, carrots smothered in a rich gravy. There were also two yeast rolls and a small plate with a piece of apple pie.

"This is lunch?" She questioned.

"Kind of linner…" Shawn said.

"DId I sleep that long?"

"Yes, but we ran into town to grab a couple of things, and it took a bit longer than expected. So, expect dinner at around 9ish." Shawn said.

Mellie looked at the clock and it was currently 3:00pm. She needed to get to work. This trip wasn't going to plan, book, or pay for itself. She didn't get the chance to pay for things often. Her family wouldn't let her. It didn't make any sense as she was incredibly well off. She threw on a sun dress, grabbed her laptop and climbed back into bed. She ate as she searched for flights for the trip. They needed a place that would hold six. It needed to be close to the Islands, but she wasn't sure she wanted to stay on the island. She'd always wanted to travel there but hadn't had the chance.

"Hey, you never told me what caused you to be not as upset about this whole situation." Shawn said. "You don't have to tell me if you don't want to, but I'd love to know what happened while you took a bath that made you seem more ok with this."

"Well, besides the fact that we're going to Scotland. Thanks for that by the way! She came to me Shawn. The Eternal Lady. She's in my head. Like how you, Dad, and Grandpa can talk to me while we're shifted. She can do it whenever she wants."

"Are you serious!?" Shawn was surprised.

"100% serious. It's hard to understand her sometimes because of the strong Scottish accent. But she seems so sweet and willing to help. I can talk back to her the same way. Also, I made sure she wasn't going to be around all the time. You know, during intimacy and such." Mellie said.

With that Mellie got back to work. It took her around an hour, but she got everything worked out. The round trip with United Airlines was booked easily enough. Then she rented a home in Brae for the two weeks. Thinking about it she knew they would need a car. So that was the next thing on her to do list.

As she was looking for a car she marveled at how cheap it was to rent one. The one issue she was having was finding a car to fit 6 people. She didn't want to rent two cars. This needed to be a family adventure all around. So, by the time she was done she found the perfect SUV. It held 7 people so everyone should have enough room. The best part was that it was only $72 a day. The total for this trip was going to be around $9,000. She quickly and quietly paid for everything. To find everything she was looking for took her until roughly mid afternoon.

When she walked outside, she had the look of accomplishment on her face. They knew she had taken care of it all and Aileen looked a bit irritated.

"You shouldn't have done all that. We could have helped." She said to Mellie.

"I know. But I wanted to do it. You guys always take care of everything and this time I wanted to help. Don't worry though. You can cover all the costs when we get there. Food, adventure, gas. The whole nine yards." Mellie said.

CHAPTER TWENTY-ONE

For the next week and a half they trained and ate and enjoyed each others company. Each night ended with an amazing time around the bonfire. The morning they packed up was bitter sweet. They were all so excited for the next leg in this adventure, but they didn't want to leave the beauty of this place. Mellie had been talking about this trip for days. She had no idea what to expect which was par for the course lately. Everyday was a mystery. Some days she woke up with golden eyes but many days when she looked in the mirror her eyes were glass blue. At least she wasn't having to shave her unibrow constantly. She had gotten closer to Shawn over these last two weeks than she ever dreamed she would have. They woke up and made love, they showered or took a bath together after each training session, they hiked every trail in the park, and loved every second they spent together. For some reason she was still so unsure if it was real. She never felt good enough for anybody and all of the sudden she was in an all encompassing relationship with a man she had been friends with forever. It didn't make sense, but again nothing in life did at the present time. She desperately hoped this trip would change that. She needed to know what and who she was.

After loading up, they headed straight to the airport. They were taking their flight out of John Glenn International airport in Columbus. This trip took them roughly an hour. They arrived at the airport at 6:30am for their 8o'clock flight. The airport was bustling with people traveling for their summer vacations. Mellie was glad it was a fast trip to the airport and even happier that they got there early.

It took them all of an hour to check their bags and go through the security check point. When they finally got to their gate, they only had twenty minutes before first boarding call. They hoped the flight wouldn't be too long and they really hoped they would have time to rest. When it was time to board, they shoved their carry-ons in the over head compartments after finding their seats. They had three two seat window rows. Shawn happily gave Mellie the window seat.

"Hey babe, mile high club later?" Shawn joked.

"You're out of your mind! The two of us wouldn't fit in these tiny bathrooms. However, ask for a blanket and maybe we can have some fun right here." Mellie joked back.

"You better not!" Mom yelled from behind them. She then added quietly, "I don't want to hear anything you two do, and since that's not possible you shouldn't subject anyone else to it either."

Mellie and Shawn died laughing. Amelia wasn't wrong. They were very loud and had been the butt of many jokes about it the whole time they were in the cave.

"Ok, Mom. You're no fun." Mellie laughed. She laid her head on Shawn's shoulder and was asleep before the plane even took off.

The flight took roughly ten hours. It was the longest any of them had ever been on a plane and it was exhausting. By the time they landed everyone was ready for a good night's sleep. Lucky for them it was the middle of the night when they got there. They took a rideshare to a little inn not far from the airport. Callem had booked rooms there while they were on their flight. They needed to stay close to the car rental place. It was the most stereotypical Scottish inn Mellie had ever seen. A two story brick building painted white. There were red brick accents and ivy climbing up the walls. It had to be the oldest building on the road. When they entered they weren't sure they were in the right place. The first floor was a dark and dingy pub that smelled of stale beer and dust. The walls were dark wood. There were pictures all over the walls of people sitting in or standing outside the pub. They were mostly old pictures in black and white. As it was the middle of the night the pub was empty, except for one man who Mellie assumed was the owner. He was a short stout man with snow white shoulder length hair and a long beard of the same color. He walked up to Mellie and Shawn.

"Awright, welcome ta' Briarwood Bar and Grill. Howfur kin ah hulp ye th' nicht? A'm Fergus." The man said with a tired smile.

"We've booked some rooms for the night." Shawn said as he wondered if he was responding to what the man said. He didn't think it mattered much but he didn't want to be rude.

"Ah, aye. A've bin expecting ye. Let me git th' keys. Ah will shaw ye tae yer rooms 'n' shaw ye th' bathroomo." Fergus said as he disappeared through a curtain. The rest of the party had just walked in. "Follow me this wey." Fergus yelled through the curtain.

They followed the man through the curtain and up an old yet well-made set of stairs.

"Ye'v git rooms 2-4 'ere. Th' bathroom is juist down the hall. Ye'll hae to use the same bathroom. Good news is, no oneelse is staying 'ere." Fergus said as he handed them their keys.

"Thank you so much for your kindness." Mellie said with a smile. The man looked at her like he knew her or knew of her. For some reason that didn't scare her it just made her curious.

"Mak' sure your down at 9am sharp fur breakfast. Tis included wi' th' room." Fergus said as he walked away.

"Alright I'm off to bed, that flight killed me." Angus said. They all said their goodnights and headed to their rooms.

The rooms were modest with big wooden framed beds. There was one skinny tall dresser in the corner, a small table and a chair in another corner and a bench at the foot of the bed. Mellie and Shawn barely spoke as they shed their clothes and hopped into bed. They curled up around each other and dozed off to sleep immediately.

Their alarm went off at 7:00am. Mellie slowly crawled out of bed and threw on a nightgown. She stumbled her way to the smallest bathroom she'd ever seen. A stand alone shower was in one corner, and a flush chain toilet next to a small pedestal sink in another. It was cute and quaint. She showered quickly in order to give everyone else the chance. By 8:50am everyone was showered and packed and headed downstairs. They left their bags on the inn side and walked into a very full pub/restaurant. Fergus had left a table for six in the middle empty for them. They all sat down and before they could even settle, the sweetest old lady was bringing them coffee, and water.

"Thank you so much. Is there a menu?" Amelia asked.

"Nope! We'll brimg you all true Scottish breakfast with all the fixings. Mah names Bonnie 'n' Fergus is ma husband." Bonnie said with a smile.

"Thank you, we look forward to it." Angus said.

They only had to wait about ten minutes before six huge piled plates were in front of them. The plates were stacked high with black pudding, haggis, square sausages, tattie scones, back bacon, fried eggs, baked beans, fried tomatoes, mushrooms, toast and tea. It was the most food they'd seen in weeks, and they weren't mad about it. Everything was very different from what they ate in the United States but so good. No one left even a drop of food. It was unfortunate that they couldn't stick around and enjoy their time in this little town, but they had to get their car and head to their AirBnb. The real adventure would begin tomorrow. Mellie would find out what she was and where she came from. Most importantly to her, where and why Morrigan went away the first time.

CHAPTER TWENTY-TWO

It was a short walk to the car rental place. They were still very happy that Fergus let them keep their bags there. It was incredibly hilly. As they were walking, people kept looking at Mellie like they knew her. She even heard things like. 'She looks juist lik' Morrigan', 'That cannae be her kin it?', 'She haes her eyes doesn't she?'. The one that would always stick with Mellie came from a little girl, no older than six. She was staring at Mellie while pulling on her moms hands.

"Maw, awright maw! She looks juist lik' th' eternal lassie doesn't she?

She haes tae be her."

"Och dear, that cannae be her. She's bin gaen a lang time. She does hae her eyes though." The little girl's mother said as she pulled her along. She looked back a couple times, shook her head and kept going.

"Grandpa, it's like they all know who I am. I don't even know who I am. Maybe before we leave, we can come back to this little town, and I can talk to some of the people here. Everyone seems to know far more than me." Mellie said.

"I think that's a grand idea." said Angus. It was like he was already picking up the Scottish accent.

Mellie smiled and put her arm through his. This had become such a incredible adventure, and she was sure she would find out who and what she was before the two weeks were up, and they went back to the real world.

It wasn't long before they arrived at the shop and their car was ready and sitting outside. It was spacious, which made Mellie happy. She was very nervous that it wouldn't be big enough. Not only were there six of them but the men were all quite large in stature. Callum went in, signed some papers and got the keys. They had decided days ago who would drive. Angus was the only one with enough left lane driving experience, so it was a no-brainer. They all got into the vehicle and started back to the inn to grab their things.

When they arrived at the inn it was a whole different vibe. The breakfast guests had left and now there were tables of young and old men sitting around with pints and what seemed like good conversation. Mellie walked up to Fergus and tapped him on the shoulder.

"Awright lassie, sin ye left tae git th' motor we haven't been able to stop thinking ye'r someone we know from long ago." Fergus said with his arm around her shoulders.

"The Eternal Lady?" Mellie questioned. When she said it, her eyes changed slowly to blue.

"Aye dear! Yer her! But howfur 'n' what took so lang? We loue ya 'n' need ye 'ere. We sing songs about yer return bit ne'er thought it wid happen." Fergus said with tears in his eyes.

"I don't know much honestly. It's all very new to me. That's why we're here. We need answers. I know nothing of what or who I am. Not sure about staying here, but I'd love to be able to come back often." Mellie said with love in her eyes.

"Ye'll fin everything yi'll need to know between 'ere 'n' Shetland. Ye come back as often as ye lik' 'n' ye'll aye hae a home 'ere." Fergus said before hugging her tightly.

When Mellie got back to the car with the bags she started to cry.

"Mom, they all know who I am. They love me. At least Fergus does. He said I'll find everything out between here and Shetland. He invited me to come back whenever and for however long I wanted. Said I'd always have a home here." Mellie was full blown sobbing with relief at this point.

Callum and Angus hugging each other and then Mellie. Shawn wrapped his arm around her and wiped the tears away with the other hand. And with that they started on their journey to the Shetland Isles.

CHAPTER TWENTY-THREE

The drive was both beautiful and scary. There were beautiful trees and hills everywhere. The greenest grass they had ever seen. The Air BnB was on the mainland and the trip wasn't very long. It was exhausting though. Mellie and Shawn sat in the back cuddled up. They talked a little about how Mellie was feeling with all the love she received at the little inn. Then without much warning she fell asleep. Well, kind of.

"Th' folk here will love ye. Ah mist warn ye though, Whin ah wis 'ere thare was a group of men that tae hurt me. In th' end thay murdurred me. I'm not sure if their family is still here or even like them, bit please be careful." Morrigan warned.

'How will I know where and who they are? Everyone in the town we stayed at last night knew me. Will they know me?" Mellie questioned nervously.

"They're nat smart folk, but ah wid suggest sunglasses at a' times. Yer eyes are the windows to th' soul. Your eyes are so much like mine. If they look they will fin' ye. Hopefully word hasn't gotten oor yit."

With that Mellie woke up. She didn't say anything, she just started rummaging through her bag. She pulled out her glasses and put them on. She wasn't sure what she'd do when she had to go into a building. She was guessing a hat would also work, so that would probably be what she wore most of the time.

They arrived at their AirBnB and were in awe. When they pulled up the driveway there were glass walls everywhere. It was incredible how much light was going into the house. They got out, grabbed their bags and walked up to the door. Mellie pushed in the code she had been sent, and they walked into what would be her favorite place in the house. The ceiling was at least twenty feet tall, and one wall was floor to ceiling windows. There were comfy chairs spread through out and a place where they would be eating at a cute little table and chairs. Through an archway was the rest of the house. It wasn't underwhelming, but nothing compared to the room of windows. They all found their bedrooms and started to unpack.

Shawn walked up behind Mellie and wrapped his arms around her.

"Hey babe, what happened while you were sleeping? You woke up still curled next to me, but you were almost frantic." Shawn asked with love in his voice.

"She spoke to me again. She told me most people would love me. There is however one group of men on the islands that will hate me. They tried to hurt her once, and that's who ended up killing her. She knows we don't look alike but says that my eyes speak volumes. They'll know as soon as they look into my eyes. I need sunglasses or a hat pulled low whenever we are in public."

"Wow, that's both good and bad news. I'm happy so many people are going to support and love you here. I don't want to have to fight a group of men though. Do you know if their family line is still here?" Shawn asked.

"I'm not sure. She gave me a picture of what the men looked like in my head. I should get a good idea just by looking around if they are still here. They may also not hold the hate for Morrigan in their hearts anymore. I'm going to pray that that is the case." Mellie hugged Shawn and kissed his chest.

They spent the rest of the day enjoying the house. The bedrooms were all so far away from each other tonight would be fun. At least Mellie hoped that her and Shawn could make love. She had been burning for him for what seemed like days. Every time they touched, she was soaking wet. She hadn't even told him, but she knew he could see it in her eyes. They needed tonight to be special.

"Hey I'm going to go take a shower and get ready for bed. I love you all so much. Shawn, give me an hour and then come up. I want to to give you a present." Mellie said after they had finished dinner and cleaned up.

Mellie and Shawn had told everyone about what Morrigan had told Mellie. They were all prepared to keep her safe.

"I'll be up then my love." Shawn said with a smile and a wink.

Mellie took the entire hour. She did an everything shower. Double face wash, double hair wash and conditioner, double body wash and shaved everywhere important. She learned Shawn liked it that she had pubic hair. She loved that. She slipped into bed wearing the sexiest thing she had brought. It was black and lace. It covered her whole body except for hole for her tits and no crotch to be found. She knew Shawn well enough to know even with all the important bits cut out he was going to rip it off her, which is exactly what she wanted.

When Shawn came up, he looked at her and did a double take. He had never seen this before and he needed to touch it. He cursed and ran to the shower. It was the fastest, and hopefully still effective shower she'd

ever seen him shower. He didn't bother drying his body or putting anything on. Shawn walked up to her very slowly and jumped on her.

"You, kitten, can't do this to me! It's been days and I need you right now. You had to put this thing on, which is beautiful and sexy but now I have to tear it off. I need to get to all of you." Shawn said with a growl.

"I was hoping you'd say that." Mellie winked. Without a second though Shawn ripped her outfit down the middle and slid it off her legs.

He began by her feet. Kissing and licking her ankles and calves. She was writhing in please by the time he got to her sweet spot, but he passed it up. Shawn continued to lick and kiss all the way up to her lips. When their lips meant it was like a fire. The way he took over her mouth was unlike anything she'd ever experienced. It was like she was the best thing he'd ever tasted. Shawn was always good with his mouth but this was different. It was almost a mutual claiming. He was hers and she was his. Forever. She loved what was happening but needed more. She put both of her hands on his shoulders and slightly yet firmly pushed him down. She stopped when his mouth reached her left nipple. He licked and sucked and bit until she moaned out in pleasure.

"More! Please!" She begged. He moved to the right side and did the same. By the time he had reached the apex of Mellie's sensitive spot she was so close to the edge it didn't take long for her first climax. As she screamed, he positioned his body and with one hard thrust he was all the way in. She instantly came again.

"Oh My God! You feel so good inside me. Like you've always belonged here." Without a second's notice Mellie had flipped him over and she was now riding him. Her head was thrown back and she continued to increase her speed. Right before he came, she hopped off of him and positioned herself in between his legs. Mellie brought her head down and licked the tip of his pulsing cock. He moaned as she licked her way down his shaft and took one ball after another into her mouth. She licked the underside of his balls and it drove him crazy. She loved the way she tasted on him, so this was a treat to say the least.

"Please ride me again! I need to come inside you." Shawn moaned.

"Say less." She giggled as she straddled him once again. She began to slowly move her hips in circles as she rode him. She picked up the pace when she saw his face. She didn't need any instructions as she could tell he was close. Shawn brought his hand up and started using his thumb to drag circles around her clit. They both began to writhe. It didn't take long for them to climax together. When they were spent, she flopped over and laid her head on his sweaty chest. She took her left hand and started to run her fingers through his chest hair.

"Mmmm, I never want this to end." Shawn said.

"It doesn't have to. "Mellie replied.

They fell asleep in the same position and it was the best sleep Mellie had ever had. She had a great day. Realizing how loved she was in this country made her feel incredible. She was slightly nervous about the potential family that didn't like her, but she guessed she'd cross that bridge when she got there.

While they slept, she dreamed. She dreamed of a future here in Scotland. She dreamt of Shawn and children, and often times visiting the family back in Ohio. She hadn't had a dream of the future in a long time. When she woke up Shawn was spooning her, and she nuzzled closer to him as he snored. He let out a light moan and held her closer.

"I hope this is what you want, because I can't imagine my life without you in it." Mellie said quietly.

"Anywhere with you is where I want to be." Shawn responded as he kissed her head.

She closed her eyes and slept for a couple more hours. They awoke with the smell of bacon and coffee.

"Let's shower and head downstairs. We've got a lot to do today." Shawn moaned. They climbed in the shower together and washed each other as they talked about the day.

"We need to get to the Islands and investigate. See if there are any people that have any information on me." Mellie said.

"Remember, we have to be careful. There may be people there who

don't care for you. It also looks like it's going to be an overcast day. A hat is probably your best option to keep your eyes hidden. "Shawn said as they dried off.

They got to the kitchen at the perfect time. Amelia had just placed all the food on the table, and the coffee and tea were both ready.

"Good morning. Sorry we slept in. We knew we were going to need rest before we got this busy day underway. "Mellie said.

"It's ok sweety. It'll be a wonderful day. We'll head to Lerwich after breakfast and catch the ferry over to the Isles." Angus said.

"That's only a 15 minute drive." Callum said while handing a trucker hat to Mellie.

Mellie went to her room and packed a bag. They would be staying on the islands for three nights. They had booked another inn, and they were very excited about it. They hoped it would mean the same warm welcome. They got in the car and headed to the ferry location.

The closer they got to the ocean the cooler it got. It was a very beautiful day but windy. Mellie realized that the hat wouldn't last long the way it was currently. She dug around for a hair tie in her bag and put her hair in a ponytail. Then stuck the ponytail through the snapback and it was secure. When they reached the ferry gate a young man stood there to write down names.

"Awright, whin wull ye be returning? That's all the information we need." The young man said.

"For now, we'll be returning in three days. If it changes at all it'll just be an extra day. We'll call and let you know as soon as we know." Shawn said.

"Soonds guid tae me. Enjoy your time in th' Shetlands." He said warmly.

"Thank you." With that they slowly drove onto the ferry and waiting for departure. It didn't take long as the only other vehicle that boarded was a delivery truck and a small sports car. With that they were on their way.

What they didn't know was that the ferry ride would take upwards of twelve hours. They were glad they booked an extra day at the inn, and also very glad that they were in an incredibly comfortable vehicle with room to sleep. They took some time to enjoy the ferry from the deck and the bathroom was big and spacious, but it was a long ride and about halfway through

Shawn started to get seasick. It wasn't bad but Mellie was glad she packed dramamine. He definitely benefited from it.

The ferry arrived at the dock in the early afternoon. Still early and perfect to get to the inn, eat dinner and turn in for the night. Before they got off the ferry, they let the young man know they would take that extra day. He nodded his head at them and watched them drive away. When they were far enough away that they couldn't see him, he pulled out his phone and made a call.

"Th' eternal lassie is back. She's wi' her fowl 'n' headed yer wey. If a'm guessing right, she'll be at the Inn soon." With that he hung up.

CHAPTER TWENTY-FOUR

It didn't take long to get to the inn, and it was stunning. White brick again but this time it was all ground level.. The wind had worn a lot of the paint off the bricks which Mellie thought gave it character. There was one larger center building which she was sure was the pub. Then off to either side were little cottages the equivalent of hotel rooms, ten on each side. They found a parking spot around back and walked into the pub from the back door. It wasn't full but there were quite a few people inside. Shawn walked straight to the bar and started a conversation with the man at the bar. He was in his early 40's and had a big muscular build,with dark hair on his head and a small beard. His eyes were brown and sad looking.

"Hi We booked three rooms last week. We'll be here for three nights." Shawn said.

"Ah aye, we've bin waiting fur ya'll. Yer rooms ur side by side at the end on the right. Rooms 18-20.Why don't you have a seat. We'll bring out a cuppa before you go in fur th' nicht." The man said.

They sat down at two tables that had been pushed together. A woman around the same age as the man came through a curtain with glasses and a pitcher of water.

"Here's some water. Whit kin ah git ye tae drink? We'll bring oot bread 'n' butter. It should be done any minute. Twa options, chicken or beef?

They decided they'd all have chicken, and some tea to warm their bones. When the lady brought out the tea she was followed by the man from behind the counter with plates piled high with food.

"A'm Archie 'n' this is ma wife Isla. We own the Wilson Inn 'ere. Tis bin passed doon fur generations oan her side. We're sae happy ye'r 'ere. If yi'll need anythin' let us ken." Archie said.

"Thank you so much. Everything looks delicious. We're as happy to be here as you are to have us." Callum said.

Their plates were piled high with roast chicken, roasted potatoes, gravy, carrots and Yorkshire pudding. They had beautiful homemade bread and freshly churned butter in the middle of the plate. After they ate Isla brought out a wonderful Cranachan for each of them. It looked like a trifle but was made with such care. Berries, honey and whiskey layered with fresh cream. They ate until they had food up to their eyeballs, and then retired to their rooms.

Mellie was happy with how the day had gone and couldn't wait for tomorrow. That was when the real work would begin. They grabbed their bags and changed into their pajamas. They slid into bed and fell fast asleep. Well, most of them did. Mellie tossed and turned all night with the voice of Morrigan in her head.

"Ye've met some o' thaim awready. Be careful, quaistion them like you will anybody else. Dinnae let thaim ken wha you are. Ah haven't sensed they know who you are yit." Morrigan said.

"Thank you but will you let me sleep now." Mellie thought-asked.

"Aye. Rest yer body 'n' yer mynd. Ye wull hae a long couple of days. Guid or bad, Naesure yit." Morrigan said and then even she rested.

Mellie snuggled into Shawn and fell asleep instantly.

They woke up surprisingly energized. It was going to be a day. They weren't sure if it was going to be a good one or a bad one. But it was undoubtedly going to be a day. Mellie had been trying to train herself to be calm in all situations. She knew that if she felt too much of any emotion her eyes would flash blue. She didn't want to have to cover her face all the time. Hopefully today would be a good indication if she was ready or not. She hadn't had to train this way before. It wasn't something anyone was used to. She secured her hat the way she had the day before. The hat wouldn't be out of place today since it was supposed to rain often. She knew the way she secured it would make it easier to pull off indoors. Today they planned on walking the town, taking in the scenery and visiting any historical places. The library was on the list, and they also intended on going to the historical society. There may be books or at least people to talk to about her history.

When the family entered the pub their table from last night was set up and ready for them. They loved that staying in these sort of Inns made breakfast cheap and included enough to fill them up. They sat down and Isla brought out coffee and scones right away.

"This is juist tae git ye stairted. Th' rest o' yer breakfast wull be oot shortly. Whit are you planning for th' day?" She asked Mellie specifically.

"Well, first of all. Thank you so much for the hospitality, and the food has been amazing. Today we are going to sightsee. Focusing mainly on the historical spots. We plan on going to the historical society and checking out our lineage. My grandparents here are first generation Americans. Other than a couple visits to the main land in their lifetime we don't know much about where we come from." Mellie answered honestly.

"Th' historical society wull be a great place tae stairt. They hae sae many books about oor bonny island. Mak' sure ye go talk to Mairi. She lives down the road 'n' happens tae be mah mither in law. Her folk haes bin 'ere fur whit seems lik' forever." Isla responded.

"Thank you so much for the tips. We will surely stop by and talk with her. If not today, then tomorrow. Mellie said.

Just then Archie walked up with plates piled high with food once again.

" 'ere ye go. Enough tae keep ye full oot oan yer adventure." He said with a smile.

It was very reminiscent of the meal that Fergus had made for them a couple days prior. They dug in.

Isla said to Archie, "Ah tellt thaim to stop by yer moms house 'n' ask her aboot th' history o' th' toun."

"Whit a great idea. She loues getting guests. 'N' only chance tae talk aboot th' history 'ere haes her excited juist thinking aboot it." He said with a chuckle.

"Thank you again and we'll be sure to stop by." Shawn said. He was being polite, but he was hoping they'd go away so they could really talk about their plans for the day.

A new couple had just walked in, so Isla excused herself to serve them. Across the room, Shawn saw Archie pick up his phone. He used what Mellie had come to refer to as his 'wolfy' senses to listen in to Archie's side of the conversation.

"Ah think ye wur wrong. Ah cannae sense anythin' aboot th' lassie. Thay seem tae be nomal tourists wha hae lineage 'ere 'n' juist wantae ken th' stories. We'll be sure tae keep our eyes peeled though. Cheers again." Archie said to someone on the other end.

Shawn leaned over to Mellie, "He doesn't suspect anything. At least he doesn't anymore. You did a good job Babe. He did say he's going to keep an eye on us so maybe just continue to control yourself like you've been doing and we'll be ok." He said quietly.

"I will try my hardest. We need to make these days productive but short then. It's exhausting not letting myself feel." Mellie responded.

They ate their fill and drank as much water and coffee as their bodies would hold and they were on their way. Knowing that Mellie had to control herself to the max made their day shorter than intended. They walked to the historical society and were greeted by the kindest, elderly woman.

"Awright dears. Mah names Catriona. Whit kin ah hulp ye with today?" She asked with a smile.

"Well, my wife and I are first generation Americans. We know a lot about the main lands, but we don't know much about the isles. We'd especially love any information you have on folklore and legends." Angus said.

"Urr ye 'ere to learn about our eternal lassie? Where ye staying while ye'r 'ere?" She asked

"We're here to learn about her and any other fun things we can be taught. We are staying at the Wilson Inn." Mellie said trying to make it seem like that wasn't all they were there to learn about.

"Och dear… Don't tell thaim that's whit ye'r 'ere tae learn aboot.

Everybody, well almost everybody loved her. That folk, the Wilson's. Husband of Isla. His fowl are the ones wha murdurred her. Left her wee boys tae fend fur themselves. Thay did it though. Thay survived 'n' thay helped our wee island whin thay wur old enough tae chaynge. Or sae mah mither tellt me. She knew th' wee boys. Thay grew up th'gither." She said with a sigh. "Things got hard for them. The Wilson's tried their hardest to get rid of them to. They have so much hate. One dae they were just gaen. We dinnae ken where they went. A'body hoped they'd continue tae hulp wherever thay wur." She had tears in her eyes. "They did continue to help. We are still helping when and wherever we can." Angus said while looking at Callum.

The woman didn't look up, she just grabbed the men and held them. Like she had known them her whole life. Maybe she wished she had.

Angus took her hand with his left hand, placed his right hand on her chin and lifted it so they were looking into each others eyes. "My father told me about a little girl that he was friends with. Your name sounded familiar. Could it be you?"

"It's me. Ah hae missed yer fowl sae much. Yer faither Callum… He must be gone by now." She responded

"He is gone. Only a couple years ago though. He was very fond of you. He had many stories to tell. May I introduce you to my family?

"Please." she said with tears streaming down her face.

"This is my wife, Amelia. Her family lived here once as well. Do you remember the Grays?" Angus asked.

"Ah did ken th' Grays. Thay a' moved o'er th' muckle pond th' same time yer fowl did if ah'ament mistaken."

"You're right. This is our son Callum, named after my father. This is Callum's wife, Aileen and their daughter Mellie. The first woman in our lineage since Morrigan. And this is Shawn, Mellie's beloved." When Angus was done with introductions Catriona walked up to Callum and just hugged him.

"You have a name that everyone here will know. They loved your da" She giggled.

"That's good to know. I'm glad that people here loved us." Callum responded.

"Loved you aye! Loved your whole family. Callum was one of my best friends." She laughed.

Mellie walked up to Catriona and placed her hand on her shoulder. She had taken her hat off and when Catriona looked up, she almost fainted.

"Ye'r her! Ah cannae believe th' stories wur true. Thare wis a legend that said Morrigan tellt th' men wha murdurred her that she would be back. Ye'r 'ere! Yer free to be yourself in this house. But when your outside please hide your identity. Especially whin ye'r at th' Inn. The will not lik' that ye'r back here. Th' Wilson's are indifferent. It's the Brown's ye'll have to look out fur. Sae ye'r 'ere tae learn aboot wha yer aren't ye?" Catriona asked.

"That is why I'm here. We had the best welcome on the mainland. Everyone seemed to be more than ok with who I am. I didn't even try to cover up. I am scared here though." Mellie said to the old woman.

"Dinnae ye worry. Ye'v git th' whjolel island tae protect ye. Ah wull plan a pairtie. No one likes the Brown's so they willnt be invited. We'll introduce ye tae a'body 'n' then thay wull watch yer back 'n' mak' sure ye'r safe. Whaur urr ye staying oan th' main land?" Catriona asked.

"We're staying at a large house we found on AirBnb." Mellie answered.

"Ye'll be safe thare. Tis big corporations that ain all those houses. Ah wis juist making sure ye wur safe." She said

"Thank you for wanting us to be safe." Shawn said puting his arm around Mellie.

"How are you handling knowing wha yur lassie is?" Catriona asked Shawn.

"Well, it was kind of an easy transition as our family are also wolves. It was a bit of a shock when Mellie changed for the first time last month and was a horse. She later changed into a wolf thanks to her dad. It's been an adjustment, but I love her with my whole heart and she can always count on me." Shawn kissed the top of her head. It made Mellie blush.

"Looks lik' ye'v found yer match. Howfur did ye deal wi' th' unexpected chaynge mah dear?" she asked Mellie

"I was so scared for the first change, but it was really easy. Changing from a horse to a wolf was even easier. No one thought I'd even be a shifter because there hadn't been a female in our family line for generations. I am so happy now that I'm used to it. My eyes change to blue when emotions hit.. That's why I am trying to train myself to not be emotional and also why I am wearing the hat." Mellie just let the words pour out. It was like she had known this woman her entire life.

Amelia touched Angus on the shoulder.

"Don't you think we should head back? I know you need some rest and Mellie looks like she's getting tired as well."? she asked.

"Gie it one more hour. Then ye dinnae hae tae come up wi' an excuse fur bein' back sae earlie. Ah will caw the kettle oan 'n' we'll hae some cuppa. Ah juist teuk some cookies oot o' th' oven." Catriona said.

"I like that idea. We'll get back just in time for dinner and then we can turn in for the night." Mellie said.

They sat and talked for over an hour. They talked about the families on the island and how close they were to one another. Catriona let them know that the reason everyone thought the Brown's didn't like them is because they basically had a monopoly on the island. They owned most of the properties and businesses and wanted to keep it that way. The people in the town that lived in poverty did so because they didn't want to work with or for the Brown's. It started what the little island described as a war, and that is when Morrigan died.Time passed so quickly. When they thought they had been there long enough to stop questions from arising they all stood up.

"It was so nice getting to know you and our family history. Thank you so much for taking all this time." Mellie said.

"'Twas mah pleasure. A'm going to send oot an invite tae th' pairtie th'morra. It'll be 'ere. Ah wid ask that ye shaw up aroond 5. That wey ye'r nae stuffed from tea. We wull hae sae a good time! Ah cannae wait tae talk mair 'n' introduce ye tae a'body." Catriona said.

They all gave her a sweet hug and headed off to the Inn. When they entered dinner was just getting started.

CHAPTER TWENTY-FIVE

T hey all chose to eat the Shepards pie that night and as expected it was amazing. In the States it was made with ground beef which was fine but in Scotland… Oh my like Haggis was everything they thought it would be. They were just finishing their meal when Isla walked up to them with tea and a plate of cookies, or as they called them biscuits.

"Did ye hae a guid adventure?" she asked. Then she continued. "Na time tae go see Mama Brown th'day? If I know anything it's that Cat kept ye strowed a'day. She sure is a talker."

"She did keep us busy all day. We did learn a great deal. Though it was quite nice." Mellie answered.

"Please say ye'll see mah mither in law th'morra. She wull tell ye our towns entire history."

"That's our plan tomorrow after breakfast. We're busy tomorrow evening though. Catriona has invited us over for dinner. So we won't be here until late I think." Mellie said

"Ya'll have fin! She likes tae git her friends togither. Thay wull talk yur ear off though" Isla laughed.

"We can't wait! I believe that we are off to bed for the night. It's been a long day. We'll see you for breakfast. Where is your wonderful husband tonight? Isn't this a lot for you to take on by yourself?" Mellie asked

"He's with his dad and brother th'nicht. He does this occasionally. Ah dinnae mynd. We hae our kitchen workers, and we haven't been busy tonight." Isla said.

"Well, that's good to hear. I'm glad you have help if you need it. It was wonderful talking to you again. See you in the morning." Shawn said.

"'Twas guid talking tae ye a' tae. See ye th'morns morning." Isla said with a smile as she walked away.

When they got back to their rooms, they were quiet.

"Isn't it strange staying here tonight know that this is the family who killed Morrigan?" Shawn asked.

"Strangely enough she doesn't seem to bothered by it. I bet it's because so many people here have my back. Back then she was the only shifter. Now besides Mom and Grandma it's all of us. She knows that you guys keep us safe. Not to mention everyone else in this town who also loves who we are. I truly can't wait for this party tomorrow." Mellie said as she flopped down on the bed.

Shawn laid down behind her and wrapped her in his arms. They were too tired to even change out of their clothes tonight. They weren't even laying on the bed right, but that didn't matter either. Sleep came fast and it was a deep sleep.

Before they knew it someone was knocking on their door. Mellie quickly stood up and opened the door. No sooner had the door opened than someone covered her head and she was carried to what she assumed was the trunk of a car and thrown in. The car sped away before Shawn even had time to blink. Shawn picked up his phone and looked at the time. It was only 3:00am. He didn't know what to do. He dialed local emergency services and let them know what had happened, then he ran to Angus and Callum's rooms. They woke up the ladies and gave them a quick run down. Told them not to worry, and away they ran. The ladies hopped out of bed and ran down the stairs to follow the guys.

They ran into the office and tried to wake up Isla and her husband. Isla finally came out rubbing her eyes and carrying a baby on her hip.

"Someone took Mellie!" Shawn yelled. "Where's your husband?"

"Whit dae ye mean teuk her? He didnae come hame. This happens whiles whin he's wi' his fowk. Thay drink and talk and usually he passes oor thare. He'll be back th' morns mornin." She said exhausted.

"Do you know who we are?" Shawn asked.

"A'richt calm doon. Dae ah ken who you are? Only what ye'v tellt me. Mah husband 'n' his fowk think ye'r family tae someone wha lived 'ere years ago. Ah dinnae know what happened to Mellie." Isla said scared.

Well, Angus said. "We are them and she is who they think she is. We just came to learn about her. We don't want any trouble and now they've taken her. Where would they take her? Is there someplace they would go that is kind of private?"

"Thir's a farm hoose abbot ten miles awa'. Tis th' only house th' cuid hae gone to. Please say thay aren't hurting her. A've ne'er understand how come thay hate her sae much." Isla said with fear in her voice.

"Don't be afraid dear girl." Callum said. "You've done nothing wrong. We have to go get her back. Please make sure our wives are safe."

"Ah wull 'n' a'm sorry." She said crying.

"You have nothing to be sorry about. Here's my number. If you hear from them, call me." Shawn said.

They didn't take their car. They may only shift with the moon during the summer but they were always fast, and their senses would work better with them in the open. It didn't take long for them to catch on to Mellie's scent. They ran as fast as they could. About halfway there Angus stopped.

"I'm going to go get Catriona. I know there are people that will help us. She can surely get in contact with her friends. We'll be better with a larger group." Angus said.

"Smart idea. We'll wait here and make sure we don't lose the way. Please be careful and hurry." Callum said. "That's my baby."

"I know son. She'll be ok. We'll get her back." Angus promised.

Catriona was already awake by the time Angus got there. It was like the woman expected him. She opened the door and ushered him in.

"Please help us. Someone took Mellie. We know who it is but want more people to help. Can you get anyone together with it being the time it is?" Angus said out of breath.

"Ah cuid tell that something wis wrong. A've awready called anyone that is of able body. They're oan thair wey. A've git something 'ere fur ye, Callum 'n' young Shawn. It'll git ye tae your full strength. You'll need all you can get fighting these guys." Catriona said.

"Are you a witch or something?" Angus asked.

"Nobody's called me a witch in a lang time. Ah kind o' lik' it. Ah guess ye cuid say that. Ah sense hings whin they're not quite right. Ah fix thaim whin ah kin. Tonight I sense you'll need your strength."

Angus pocketed the pills she had handed him. He would use them when they were all together. He had just placed them in his pocket when there was a heavy knock on the door. When Catriona opened it ten large young men walked in.

"Whit kin we help with tonight teacher? We heard yer call 'n' cam as fleet as we cuid." One of the men said.

"Morrigan is back lik' she said she wid be. Someone teuk her th' nicht 'n' she's in danger. This is her grandpa. Follow him, he'll leid ye tae her. Ye wull need tae be pure, tough 'n' brave." Catriona said.

"As ye wish teacher." said the young man.

Angus didn't look back, he just ran. Callum and Shawn were waiting on him when he returned. The men that followed were as big as houses, but they were as quiet as mice. Angus took the pills out of his pocket and handed them to Shawn and Callum.

"Catriona is a witch. She was waiting when I got there. Said she could feel that something wasn't right. She had already called these men. They call her teacher. I think that she has been preparing for this for years. She told us to take these. They will bring us to our full strength. I think that it means we'll be our wolf selves a little early in the month boys." Angus swallowed his imediately. Callum and Shawn followed.

It worked instantly, but not exactly how they thought it would. Shawn became his normal black wolf, but he could feel a strength he didn't know he had. Callum and Angus on the other hand because their Wulver selves. Half wolf half man but enormous. It put their regular wulver selves to shame. They wasted no time.

"Let's go boys!" Yelled Callum to the men that had come to help. It took them no time to reach the farm. They figured they wouldn't be in the house, but that was the first place they checked. They had the human men run through the house. It was empty as expected, except for one boy. He tried to scream, but one of the men tapped on his mouth and his lips instantly sewed themselves shut. When they left the house they immediately ran to the out buildings. There were five so they divided and conquered. People were working in each building. They were all doing things that looked pretty illegal. They wouldn't be doing that anymore. With a swish of the arm the buildings collapsed and caught fire.

They had left the largest building for last. It wasn't locked so they walked straight in. They were not expected to say the least. The people inside were just sitting around. It was the entire Brown family including a little old lady. When she saw the group of men led by two wulvers and a werewolf she screamed. They all stood up.

While this was going on Shawn had located Mellie. She was sitting on a chair in the middle of the room bloody and bruised.

"Who did this?!" He growled. "You will pay."

"Whin we heard she had come back we didnae want to believe it. It wasn't 'til ah follaed ye tae Catriona's hoose that ah knew fur sure. She haes tae be stopped!" Isla's husband said.

"Stopped from what? All we did was come here so she could learn about what she was and where she came from." Angus yelled as he attacked. He laid one strong claw against the side of Archie's face. It took out his left eye immediately. The rest of his face would scar.

While this was happening, Shawn ran and untied Mellie. She was weak and he quickly carried her outside so she wouldn't see the carnage that was sure to ensue.

"Hey jackass!" Callum yelled. "Your wife knows what you've done. Your marriage is over. Look outside. Every building on this property is on fire. Your businesses are no longer. The man in the main house will never talk again. You've lost it all."

Mrs. Brown shrieked and broke down in tears Archie ran to her.

"Maw, urr ye a'richt?" He asked.

"It's over. It's all over. This time for good." Mrs. Brown said.

"It didn't have to be over. You murdered Morrigan and she said she'd be back. She came back not to fight, or hurt anyone, but to show love and take care of the communities around her. Just because it "messed" with your desire to destroy didn't mean you had to attack her. We were headed home in a little over a week." Angus said.

"Headed hame? Ye'r Nae gaun hame?" Mrs. Brown cried.

"Oh, I'm going home. So is Callum and our wives. I have a feeling Mellie and Shawn will be hanging around. Callum and I will be back for ten months out of every year. You will never run this town in fear again." Angus said.

Mellie limped over to him. She had to be helped as her eyes were almost completely closed up. She walked up to Mrs. Brown and without warning smacked her across the face. Mrs. Brown let out a blood curdling scream.

"I was never here to hurt you. I just wanted to know who I am, and what I am meant to do with my life. You decided to change everything. I will be aggressive only when I have to be. I suggest, that you and your family act right, treat people the way they are meant to be treated and stop stealing from the people of these islands. Now that I know what's been going on I am not leaving. I will make sure that you never hurt anyone again. Is that understood?" Even hurt Mellie stood strong.

The Browns were mostly on the floor covered in blood by the time Callum and Shawn were done with them. It was dawn before Mellie,

Callum, Angus and the men who were helping finally starteed to walk away. When Mellie looked back, she was simultaneously heart broken and satisfied. She saw nothing. Everything was burned down to the ground and the air was covered in smoke. Everything that is, except for the barn where they had beat her senseless. It was the only structure still standing. She had decided to let it stand. Despite their actions, she wouldn't leave this family completely homeless.

When they got back to the Inn Isla was waiting for them. She was a mess. All tears and anger.

" A' this time I had no idea that I was married tae someone wha cuid dae the things to a woman." She cried as she gather supplies to clean Mellie up. It was the least she could do at the moment.

"Hurting me was only the end of it. They killed Morrigan all those years ago. They kept an evil hand on these islands for years. Every bad thing that happened. People losing their houses, not having proper food, owning every business by simply stealing from the owners. They did all this. When Morrigan tried to stop them all those years ago they killed her. They left her sons to fend for themselves. They managed to survive and even helped people when they could. They didn't move to the United States until their lives and families were also in danger."

"They're th' folk wha kept us down all these years? Ah mist hae bin so blind. Thay wur mean to me bit ah juist figured tis how they were with their wives. A'm feelin' sae awful fur nae seeing it." Isla cried as she wiped the blood gently off Mellie's face.

Mellie wrapped her arms around Isla. "It's not your fault. Love blinds us sometimes. Even if it's not true love."

"Howfur am ah suppose tae run th' Inn without their help? Tis bin passed doon fur generations. Ah cannae lose it. A dinnae know what I'm going to do." Isla said as she began to put ointment on the lacerations on Mellie's face.

"I have a crazy idea." Amelia said. "You plan on staying here, right?" She asked Mellie.

"I have so much work to do here now that the Brown's are done running things. I have to stay and make sure it all get's worked out. I need to reassure people that they aren't in danger of losing their homes or businesses anymore." Mellie said confidently.

"Isla, what do you think about Mellie staying with you? She can help run the Inn and she's a great cook. That way you're not alone and have the people you need. She can work out of the office in the Inn and do for you whatever you need to do around here." Amelia suggested.

"Ah would love th' hulp. Ah don't waant Mellie tae feel obligated tae work 'ere though. Ah wouldn't want her tae be overwhelmed." Isla answered honestly, yet she remained hopeful.

"It would help me tremendously and would mean I didn't need to look for a place elsewhere. I'd love to work in the Inn. It would be the perfect place to start helping the people in this town. Also, it would mean I'm here to make sure that your husband will leave you alone. With me here he definetely won't be bothering you." Mellie said looking at Isla.

Isla began to cry again. This time it was with love and gratitude. Mellie looked up at Shawn. He looked both relieved and sad. He knew he would have to leave soon. He hadn't come on this trip thinking he'd have to leave Mellie behind. He knew that it was the right thing. Tears began to well in his eyes.

"Babe, what's going on in that gorgeous head of yours?" Mellie asked as she wrapped her arms around his waist.

"I don't want to leave you here. I fully intend on coming back but I have to make sure Dad is ok. I don't know how long I'll be gone or what I'll do without you. It's a scary prospect." Shawn said squeezing her tight.

"It won't be too long. I'll be here helping rebuild the town the Browns destroyed and when you get back, I'll have a place set up for us. A full life here, where we can help all year round." Mellie said reassuring him.

"I'll just miss you."

"I'll miss you too, but it isn't time to go anywhere yet. Let's enjoy the rest of your trip. We'll go to the Air BnB house the day after tomorrow and gather our things. We'll come straight back here and get to work. Plus, I need to go see Fergus and his wonderful family. We will spend so much time together and then you'll be back in no time." Mellie tried to reassure him.

Isla had disappeared into the back. When she came back, she had a pad of paper. She sat down and began to write on it.

"What's that list?" Mellie asked.

"A'm making a list o' all the folks the Brown's hae' bin awfy tae thaim. Maybe this afternoon we can let a'body know that thay na langer run th' toun. Reassure theim that your here hulp. And we can have a party this weekend. Catriona haes awready sent a dress ower fur ye tae wear. Tis in an old box. It wouldn't surprise me if 'twas Morrigan's." Isla told Mellie. It was like her brain was running a million miles a minute.

"We didn't know it was a fancy party. I'll have to take the family shopping. They can't go looking like ranch hands, and well, let's be honest. That's what they always look like." Mellie laughed.

Shawn pulled his face into a shocked appearance.

"Me, a ranch hand? Never. I own the ranch baby." He laughed.

"That sounds like a wonderful and productive day. I'm going to go lay down for a while." She said looking at the clock on the wall. It was only 8am.

"That sounds lik' a guid idea. Ah will start breakfast so it's ready when the patrons get here." Isla said with exhaustion in her voice.

Amelia and Aileen walked down the stairs just then. They hadn't slept through the events but they had stayed behind. They were human and would have been in danger. But now they knew how they could help. "You've got two more sets of hands right here. We've been resting and are ready to pitch in."

"YAY! Ye'v git na idea howfur muh this wull hulp." Isla said running and giving them both a quick hug. "I'd love to have you make what you traditionally have for breakfast. It's aboot time this place had a little change." Isla said hopefully.

With that the ladies got to work and Mellie and Shawn found themselves falling peacefully asleep.

CHAPTER TWENTY-SIX

When they woke up they could hear the people and smell the coffee.

Shawn wrapped Mellie in his arms and pulled her to him. She nestled her head against her chest and started to run her fingers through his chest hair.

"I'm going to miss this so much." She sighed.

"Me too Love, me too." Shawn said kissing her forehead. "I won't be gone for long. I'll be back before you know it. Lenny has been looking for work. I bet Dad will agree to keep him on at the farm. Callum will be there for a month after I return and then he'll be here, but the rest of them can surely take care of everything else."

"I know they can, and I know you'll be back. The time will pass so fast with us being so busy. This was not what I expected coming here. That I wouldn't be going home, but this place strangely feels like it's where I belong. Even more so now that I know you'll be here with me." Mellie said slowly getting up.

Mellie walked towards the mirror and was happy and surprised to see her face looked like it hadn't been mangled at all. Her eyes were blue. Which she didn't expect.

She felt Shawn's arms around her.

"You look wonderful with your blue eyes. I bet they've changed permanently now. You don't have to hide who or what you are here. You are finally free to just be you." Shawn kissed her again.

"I'm famished and I know Mom and Grandma did an amazing job. Let's go down and eat." When they walked down the stairs they were shocked at the number of people at the pub. Every seat was taken except for the two meant for them. They sat down and coffee was brought to them in an instant.

Amelia and Aileen had worked hard making a hybrid breakfast with Isla. It was the Scottish staples but they had added sausage gravy and homemade biscuits. The biscuits were new to the menu, but they could tell by the scarfing and the sounds of delight that they were a hit.

"Look Mel! They love the biscuits and gravy!" Mom said

"I never doubted that they would! Am I going to be expected to make them every morning?" Mellie asked half joking.

"Thay wull be a permanent fixture on my menu. Well, looks like I'll need your help until I learn tae make it, aye. It'll be sae much fin workin' wi' ye everyday." Isla said.

They all heard the door bell chime and looked behind them. They sat there shocked. Mellie stood up and went straight to the door. It was some of the younger Brown's.

"What the hell are you doing here?" she said with a strength she hadn't possessed before.

The Brown's backed up. "We juist cam in tae eat. Ye burned oor scullery doon mind. We aren't 'ere tae cause ony problems." Archie's cousin Byron said.

"Hey Shawn, can you pull one of the tables from the back and sit it outside. They can eat the food, but they'll not do it in the building." Mellie said firmly.

"Sure Babe." Shawn got up and started to gather the chairs first.

"Whit dae ye mean outdoors? This is ma cousin's business."

"Yer cousins? Tis mines 'n' has aye bin mines. Passed doon fur generations." Isla said standing her ground. "Ye'r na langer welcome 'ere."

"Let's let them eat." Mellie said compassionately. "They won't come into the building, but we can't let, even them, go hungry. You, Brown family are really lucky that I don't put you out back by the garbage. Understand me? One slip up and you're gone from here. You'll have to get your food elsewhere."

"A'richt... We understand. Kin ye please bring us whit a' body else is huvin?" He asked with fearful eyes.

"It'll be right out. HEY DAD? Can you make sure these people eat their fill and then get out of here?" Mellie said

"Sure, can do. This new job is going to be fun." He said laughing.

After breakfast Mellie took the list and she and Isla headed out to meet the people. Everyone knew some of what was going on, but the second they saw her eyes they knew it was true. She was greeted with love from most people, and uncertainty by others. It was better than Mellie expected, and she returned to the Inn excited to get ready for the party Catriona had planned.

Mellie spent the early afternoon shopping with the family. Getting them all out of rancher clothes was fun and challenging. When it was all said and done Angus had refused to go without his Stetson, but they all looked incredible. Mellie was the last to get ready, but she had her mom and Isla helping with her hair and makeup. She hated makeup but what Isla was doing was so light and fresh that she looked like a better version of herself. Her mom had found a stunning circlet in the bag that accompanied her dress. Aileen curled Mellie's hair and placed the circlet on her head. She pinned hair around it so it stayed secure. Mellie couldn't see it. They had taken the one and only mirror out of eye sight so she'd be surprised. Mellie slipped into a royal purple dress that hung to the ground. It had a small train, that was made of a wonderful sheer material that was so soft it was hard to not pet it. There were glass beads along every border on the dress which gave it the perfect weight. She slipped into satin lavender flats that had the same beading. It was like everything was made just for her.

When Mellie finally stood in front of the mirror she barely recognized herself. She looked just like the woman in a picture down the hall. Every bit of what she was wearing she had seen in that photo. She had never felt more beautiful. She still wore the amulet around her neck but it had changed color. It was the same clue as her eyes. The circlet on her head was stunning. There were tiny purple gems surrounded by tear shaped quartz stones. There was a big gem laying on her forehead that matched her eyes and amulet. It was like they were glowing.

"In the name of the wee man. Ye look so much lik' her. Ye wur called tae be 'ere 'n' ah cannae wait fur Catriona tae see ye." Isla said.

"I can't wait for Shawn to see you!" Mom said excitedly.

With that Mellie walked over to the Inn. Shawn, Callum, Amelia and Angus were waiting for them there. Their jaws hit the floor when they saw her.

"I have never seen a more beautiful woman in all of my life. I'm so lucky to call you mine." Shawn said kissing her lightly so as not to mess up her makeup.

"Stop, you're making me blush." Mellie said turning away.

"Tonight is all about you. I can't wait for everyone else to see Mellie, the Eternal Lady." Amelia said.

With that they walked the short distance to Catriona's house. They didn't know how but it was almost like the building had grown double in size. They did know actually, but it was not what they expected at all. They hadn't even made it to the door when it opened. Catriona stood there in an angelic white gown. She was stunning and commanded respect.

"Good evening." Mellie said as they made their way to the entrance. "look at you deary! Aren't ye a site. Th' nicht is going tae be amazing. A've bin planning this in mah head fur years 'n' th' nicht is finally 'ere. We get to welcome you home." Catriona said while gently hugging Mellie.

"Thank you for doing this. Your place looks incredible!" Mellie said

"Just wait until you see the crowd. A'body is waiting fur ye." Cat said, escorting them in.

Mellie walked in and her jaw hit the floor. There were tables with center pieces that matched her dress and eyes. There were white roses and sprigs of lavender. Blue table clothes and blue and purple tulle lining the walls and ceiling. There was a dance floor and a band set up. At one end there were tables piled with food. On the other end there was a platform that had one long table with a throne and five other seats. It reminded Mellie of a cross between a wedding and a quincenera. She had been to both many times and it was a little bit of both. The biggest difference was that it was all for her. She was something the world needed desperately and hadn't seen in hundreds of years. She was ready for this new adventure.

CHAPTER TWENTY-SEVEN

Mellie stepped out onto her porch with a mug of coffee. The days were getting short and chilly. She was wrapped in a blanket. In the months she'd been in Scotland without Shawn, she had a house built, and rebuilt most of the Islands. People were happy, healthy and self sufficient for the first time in their lives. She did rounds everyday, after helping Isla at the Inn. It wasn't to check-up on anyone, but to make sure they didn't need anything. She helped where she could and sent others to help where she couldn't. She continued to edit for the magazine. She'd even begun to write. Her boss wanted the people to know about the Islands that Mellie now called home. She loved writing this column. It even included answering questions about food, vacations, and places to stay when people came to visit. And indeed, the people came. It brought so much business that Isla had to hire on a couple extra hands.

Isla had changed drastically. She was confident and determined. She did any and everything she set her mind to. The Browns bothered no one. They'd built a much smaller main house and a shed on their old property. They were quiet and never asked for anything. Mrs. Brown had passed about a month after the kidnapping. Mellie attended the funeral with Isla and shared her genuine condolences. Isla even let the Brown's eat inside the restaurant. Mellie made sure they stayed in line.

Over these months Mellie learned more about herself than she had ever dreamed possible. With the help of Catriona and Morrigan of course. She learned that she could change whenever she wanted and into whatever she wanted. When she felt like running she would become the white horse that everyone, including her had grown to admire and love. When she wanted to check on everyone quickly and quietly, she became a beautiful white hawk and flew low to receive any treats people tossed to her. At night an owl. She hadn't needed her wolf and she was ok with that for now.

Today she was sure that would change. Callum and Shawn would be there soon, and when their wolves needed to run she would join them. She decided to head to Isla's and wait for her guys there. She spent the day washing dishes and preparing an early dinner. She was in back when she heard the door bell ding. She had a feeling she knew who would be there and she was right. She walked out of the kitchen to see her dad standing there. He looked like he was struggling to keep it together. Tonight, he would change and stay in his wolfman form for the next ten months. She ran to him and hugged him tight.

"Where's Shawn? Please say he's here." Mellie said with worry in her tone.

"He's here but he was taking a surprise to the house. We should head there now. I could use some sleep before tonight." Callum said.

They headed to the house. When they walked over a hill Mellie's heart began to race. There he was, Shawn, riding Clyde and holding the reign of none other than Bonnie! He brought them! She couldn't believe her baby was here, and the absolute love of her life of course. When they were mere feet apart Shawn jumped down and landed on one knee. Catriona walked out of the barn and stood in front of them.

"I missed you more than words can say and I never want to leave you again. I want you to be mine and I want to be yours. Will you be my wife?" Shawn asked.

Mellie began to cry. She wrapped her arms around Shawn's head.

"I had no idea this was happening! You brought our babies!" When she was done rambling she looked down and saw the ring. She had seen this ring before. She was pretty sure it was his late mothers. It was rose gold. The main stone was Moss agate, surrounded by amethyst, small moss agate, and aquamarine.

"Babe, this ring was your mothers. I can't take that." She said still shaking.

"All I need is a yes. Please say it is a yes. Yes, it was my mother's. Dad wants you to have it." Shawn responded.

"Of course it's a yes!" She cried.

Shawn slid the ring onto her finger, stood up and wrapped her in his arms.

Mellie had forgotten about Callum and Catriona when they began to clap, and cry. Mellie, without warning began to run and transformed into a horse. Shawn looked shocked. He hadn't been around when she had discovered how to make herself change not on a full moon, and he was struck dumb with her beauty. He was excited about the change tonight.

When Mellie calmed down she changed back to herself. As she returned a small crowd had formed to congratulate them. She, however, after her pre-shift shift needed a nap. After thanking everyone for their well wishes she took Shawn's hand on one side and her dad's on the other. They walked to the house and she walked straight to her bed. She had every intention of taking a nap, however, every time she came close to falling asleep she remembered what had just happened and then remembered the stunning ring on her finger.

When the evening rolled around she made her way to the living room. The men had made themselves right at home.

"I suppose we should get ready for tonight." Angus said.

No need. Everyone here knows who and what we are. They do lock their doors at night, but I honestly think its "Brown" PTSD." Mellie laughed.

"So, we're free to be wherever we want?" Shawn asked.

"Yes, my love. We are free to roam. Just don't go feral for the strays roaming around." She giggled.

Mellie walked them out to the backyard. She had built the most amazing place for the change. She, in the hills on her property, had built benches, beds and chairs to be as comfy as possible. They were hidden slightly. Mainly for the comfort of Callum. She knew houses made him nervous, at least that's what she'd thought. However, that wasn't the truth. He didn't like being around houses because he HAD to stay hidden. He appreciated the sentiment, but here he would be free.

They sat down and got comfortable. They chatted about their home in Ohio. Mellie gave them the details of their new home. They watched the sun set and started to get antsy.

"This is howfur tis suppose tae be. Freedom, with folk who want us around. A'm sae happy fur oor freish adventure mah dear." Morrigan said.

Mellie had been practicing. She decided a wolf was the way to go tonight. It didn't take long for them all to start their transformation. Mellie easily and quickly shifted into her wolf.

She was white with transparent dark blue eyes. She looked almost regal. Callum was next. Mellie had never seen this transformation before.She had seen his wolf side, and his Wulver side. She hadn't seen the Wulver transition. Instead of shifting down he grew taller. Around 7 feet. His entire body covered in auburn and brown fur. His eyes were the goldest she'd ever seen them. When Shawn began his transition Mellie was transfixed. His wolf was perfect. Jet black, long haired coat, he had bright green eyes and was huge. Not as big as Callum in his wulver form but still huge.

As soon as Shawn was fully changed Mellie pounced. He didn't stand a chance.

"Hey!" Shawn thought to her. "You can't do that. Unfair! You've practiced all these weeks." He laughed

Mellie chuckled and they began rolling in the grass. Callum was already down the hill. It had been so long since he'd had this much freedom.

Mellie nipped Shawn's neck and it was over. He began growling and instantly licked her from paw to tail, back to belly. It made Mellie purr. It was a passion unlike any she had ever experienced before. Mellie began to run. She wasn't sure why, but knew she needed to. Shawn was fast on her heals. She stopped to stretch up against a tree and didn't move. Shawn was behind her in an instant. She felt him stretch up behind her and plant his claws into the tree so their paws were touching.

"Be careful little one. You're playing with fire." Shawn said.

"Maybe I want to play with fire, my love." Mellie responded.

Shawn licked the fur right behind her ears, and Mellie's back arched. She instantly felt the pressure of him at her entrance. She purred.

"Please…" She moaned. With that Shawn entered her. It wasn't soft or gently. It was animalistic, intense, and absolutely incredible. Shawn continued to thrust into Mellie's wolf. With the intensity of their love making they heard the tree crack. Without much more warning they were now on top of the tree that had just fallen over. He continued to pound her. He bit into the spot between her shoulder and neck and she arched further back into him and started to wag her hind quarter back and forth. She could feel him getting closer, and she wanted to go at the same time as him. She started to meet every thrust. Her backwards thrusts had her front rubbing back and forth on the bark of the tree.

"I'm going to cum!" She screamed right before she came undone with a loud growl. When Shawn felt her clench around his girth he let go and came with her. They orgasmed for what seemed like an eternity. When they were finally calm enough so that he could pull from her they laid side by side and licked themselves clean. It wasn't long before they drifted into sleep. It didn't last long as it was rudely interrupted by Callum running to make sure everything was alright. He heard the tree fall and then all the wolf noises. He thought that one of them had been hurt. Color him shocked when they began cleaning each other and themselves. If he hadn't been so furry Mellie was sure she would have seen him blush. He did turn away.

As he walked away Mellie heard him mumble, "Try to find a stronger tree next time damn it." Mellie and Shawn began to laugh.

They guessed it was only midnight. They still had the whole night in front of them. Mellie led Callum and Shawn around the town. People had not only wanted them there but also wanted to feed them. It was amazing to see the amount of meat that people had left on their doorsteps. Mellie and the guys ate their fill and then Mellie quickly changed back into her human form and started to collect the rest.

"Why are you taking the meat we aren't eating?" Shawn asked.

"Well, I talked with Catriona last week about tonight. She told me about this custom. Which is what we just participated in. in the past, out kind would freely eat what the villagers had left them, but then the rest would go to waste. That wasn't going to fly in my brain. So, tomorrow after we rest we will host a cookout on our land. Dad don't even begin to worry.

They know you won't change back and they're ok with it. Just don't mind the questions. Also, Catriona specifically would like to talk to you about that sometime this week."

"Umm.. Ok." He said questioningly. They continued to help gather the meat. Mellie started to walk in the villagers gardens and pick up veggies and berries as well. When they returned back home from their food gathering Callum and Shawn fell asleep on the rock beds in the back yard.

Mellie went into the house and started to clean the food they had collected. When the sun rose with the dawn she had just laid her head on the pillow. She heard the door quietly open and close then heard light footsteps up the stairs. Shawn showered quickly then climbed into bed. He found Mellie with his arms and curled himself around her, then he drifted into sleep. They awoke to a knock on the door several hours later.

"No rest for the wicked." Mellie laughed and hopped out of bed. Shawn grumbled and covered his head with the blanket. She left him there and went to answer the door. Before she reached the bottom of the stairs a smile crept up her face.

"Good morning, Catriona. How are you feeling today?" Mellie said.

"A'm feeling great despite tae auld bones. Howfur did lest nicht gang? Ah hawp good. Ah clocked ye grabbed a' th' hings fur oor wee pairtie." Cat exclaimed.

"Yes, I had to explain to the guys what we were going to do. Dad's a little nervous for everyone to see him like this, but will always welcome a party. Can I help you with anything today?" Mellie inquired.

"Aye. A'd love to talk tae ye da afore folk turn up. He can come back to my house for a bit, if he's ok with it. Ah fun something in an auld book a'd lik' tae talk to him aboot." Catriona said.

"I'm sure he wouldn't mind. Why don't you go out with me to wake him, and he can just follow you home." Mellie said.

"Aye." and they began to walk.

CHAPTER TWENTY-EIGHT

They walked around back and down a small hill. There he was curled up under a wool blanket Mellie had given to him this morning. Mellie walked up to him and tapped him on the shoulder. He gently opened his eyes and then startled awake when he saw Catriona next to her.

"Umm," he said. "Good morning, Catriona. Please don't mind the appearance."

"Dinna worry yourself aboot it sweetheart. Tis nothing I haven't seen in mah dreams afore." She laughed.

"Catriona would like you to go to her place. She found something in a book that she thinks would really interest you. Can you go now? That way you'll be back before people arrive." Mellie said.

"Sure. As long as you don't mind me in your house like this." Callum said.

" C'moan ye stubborn jimmy. Ye'll be fine." Cat joked.

With that they set off and Mellie walked back towards the house. As she walked up the stairs onto the back porch Shawn was there greeting her with a cup of coffee.

"Good morning my soon to be wife. I hope you slept well. What is with Cal leaving with Cat?" Shawn asked.

"They're off to look at something Catriona found in a book. In the mean time we have meat to marinate and veggies to prep. Want to help?"

"Absolutely." Callum said as he bent down and lightly brushed a kiss to Mellie's lips.

"No time for that. We have a party to prep for. But find me after or maybe even during and I'm all yours." Mellie winked and walked in the house. They spent the early afternoon cleaning and prepping. They marinated the meat, and wrapped the veggies in foil. Each packet contained mushrooms, onions and asparagus. It was seasoned with salt, pepper, and oregano with a touch of olive oil. Mellie cut up enough fruit to feed an army and made a fruit salad. Shawn made a metric ton of iced tea. sweet, and unsweet, as well as fresh squeezed lemonade and some cucumber water. Mellie made four dozen cupcakes and twelve batches of cookies. She was so glad that she had chosen a double oven when she remodeled the kitchen. She made sure the bathroom off the mudroom was fully stocked and over stocked with hand soap, and rolls of toilet paper. She had just come back in the house when the front door opened and in walked Callum. Not just Callum but him in his human form.

"What?!" Mellie screamed as she ran towards her dad. "How? What?

Ummm I don't understand."

"Calm down pumpkin. Catriona found a spell in her grandmother's oldest book. It was accompanied by a letter. The letter told her that her grandmother was the one that cast the spell that made us stay transformed. It wasn't out of malice but to protect us from the Brown's. She didn't want a moment where we were in danger. She did it all this time to protect us boys. What she didn't know was that it would be passed down to every man in our line regardless of the location. She also didn't account for the event that we would leave and wouldn't be in danger anymore. Catriona let me know that she could reverse the spell and I could essentially be like you, Mellie.. I can change when I need to or want to, and don't have to hide anymore. I clearly chose that option."

Just then Mellie's phone rang. It was her mom. Mellie picked up and heard yelling.

"Mel, is your dad around? Angus just called and umm well… He's human. Is your dad ok?"

"Mom, calm down. Dad is human as well. It was a spell that was just reversed. They are safe and free to change whenever they want. I was just wondering if it had affected Grandpa as well. I guess I got my answer. Call him back and tell him to head to the farm. Also, you folks need to pack. Shawn proposed to me yesterday and now that Dad and Grandpa are human, I want you to come and celebrate with us. Maybe even a wedding soon?" She questioned looking up at Shawn.

"ANYDAY! ANY TIME!" Shawn yelled and hugged her tightly.

"Ok sweety. We'll get ready." Mom said and hung up.

"Dad does this also give you the ability to change into other animals?" Mellie asked.

"I'm not sure entirely. Something we can investigate tonight after the party."

"I'd like that very much. Shawn, not to tell you what to do but maybe you should call your dad and see if he wants to get ready to fly here. I'd love him at the wedding. We don't have a date or a venue or a dress, or really anything, but I'd love it to be soon now that it can be." Mellie said.

"Absolutely. I'm sure he'd love to. I'll let him sleep a bit more. The change has come harder for him as of late. I'll step away from the crowd during the party and give him a call." Shawn said and kissed Mellie on the head.

Mellie got the grill and smoker she had just bought out of the shed. She set them up in a clearing and lit them both. The party wouldn't start for a couple of hours, but she needed to make sure they both worked properly. She knew she wouldn't have time to smoke any meat, but she wanted to smoke her baked mac and cheese and a pineapple for the guests. She was hoping this would be a monthly thing at least. Something to bring a once broken community closer together.

CHAPTER TWENTY-NINE

It was around 7:00pm when people started to roll in. Some had baskets with food to add to the ton Mellie and Shawn had prepared. They brought chairs, tables and some brought picnic blankets. Catriona walked up with a bowl filled with Scotch eggs. Mellie was excited about the Scotch eggs, but that could wait. She wanted to say a heart felt thank you for what she had done for Angus and Callum.

"Catriona, I can't say thank you enough for giving back Dad and Grandpa a real life. We are going to try to see if he can change into anything else or if he's still just a wolf. He'll be happy either way but we want to investigate." Mellie said as she gave Cat a hug.

"Ah think that would be an amazing idea. They're both guid men 'n' ah knew when I found th' spell ah hud tae give them th' option tae be free." Catriona said hugging her back.

There must have been close to a hundred people running around Mellie's yard. She was glad she had overcooked and overstocked.

Everyone was so happy and so surprised to see Callum in human form. When the sun went down and the night began to chill Shawn built and lit a very large fire. Everyone sat around it laughing and singing old Scottish folk songs.

"I just down from the Isle of Skye
I'm no very big but I'm awful shy
All the lassies shout as I walk by,
Donald, where's your trousers?

Let the wind blow high and wink blow low
Through the streets in my kilt I go   All the lassies
cry,
Hello!
Donald, where's your trousers?"

They danced and danced and the kids laughed and laughed. It was the most amazing night. When the crowd started to dwindle, Mellie and Shawn began to clean up. Callum chased the kids around growling like he was still the wulver. The kids would scream, and laugh and keep on running. The last villager left the house and the three of them gathered around the fire that was finally starting to burn out.

"Dad, do you want to try here, so we're close by?" Mellie asked.

"Sure. I have been thinking about it all day long. I'm not sure what I should try to change into. It's so unlike anything I've ever done before. Maybe I'll try something tiny. Like a mouse." He laughed.

"Let's do it!" Mellie said smiling.

With that Callum sat down in between Mellie and Shawn. He instantly began to shrink. Before their very eyes he became the cutest little mouse. He was small and gray with the cutest little ears that were too big for his body. Tiny little beedy eyes and the cutest little mouth. Mellie picked him up and gave him a little pet on the head. Callum chuckled to himself as he transformed back into his human form while he was still in Mellie's hand. The speed at which it happened and the weight of Callum's human form made Mellie flip backwards off the bench with him on top of her. He rolled off and then continued to roll around laughing hysterically. It was the freest Mellie had ever seen him and she was so happy. Mellie decided with this new knowledge that she would call home and see how Angus was doing.

"Hey Mom! We just found out something great."

"What's that sweety?" Her mom asked.

"Well, you know that Dad and Grandpa aren't in their permanent Wulver form. We just figured out that they can change at will and into whatever they want, like me. Dad just had the best time transforming back into his human self while I held the cutest little mouse version of him in my hands. Mom, I've never seen him so happy and free." Mellie said excitedly.

"Your grandpa will be home soon. I'll tell him to turn into a barn cat so he can kill all the mice around here. As long as it's not your dad." She laughed whole heartedly. "So, when are we thinking about having this wedding?"

"Soon, now that Dad and Grandpa can be here in human form. We want to do it here. I'm thinking a month and a week out. That way it's not Shawns change night so we can enjoy the whole night together. We know there will be no family from Ohio but you guys and Shawn's dad. We've made so many friends here, so I'm almost certain the entire town will be here." Mellie said. She wanted to keep going but decided that she needed to let Mom process.

"That sounds like a great plan. Do you know what you're going to do about a dress?" Mom asked.

"I am having the local seamstress make my dream dress. I want you to be a part of that. I was wondering if you could bring your dress and we can make some of mine out of some of yours?" Mellie asked hopefully.

"I would love to bring it! I was hoping when the day came you would be willing to at least use parts of the ugliest dress in history." She laughed.

"Mom! It's not that bad." Mellie said.

"Mellie! We've laughed until we almost peed just looking at pictures. It was that bad. I don't know what I was thinking. I don't know why your dad didn't run right out of that church." She laughed. "Speaking of church where do you think you'll be having the wedding?"

"I'm thinking on my property. I have a lot of it and there's the perfect spot under some trees. Catriona will be performing the wedding so no church. It'll be great and beautiful." Mellie said. "I have to get off here. It's very late. I'm going to book your flight in the morning."

"Alright love. I'll talk to you soon. Call me about the flights. I love you."

Mellie went straight in the house and pulled up her laptop. She booked a flight for her mom, grandma, grandpa and Shawns dad. It wasn't going to be nearly as expensive as the last time because it wasn't as last minute. She did want them there in a couple weeks so she made that happen. They would be staying with her so lodging wasn't an issue. Just when she had finished she heard Shawn and her dad walk in. Shawn walked up to her and peeked over her shoulder.

"Why do you do that?" He asked sadly. "I know that you have the ability and the funds but why don't you ever ask me to help? You're not alone anymore my dear and you never will be."

"She leaned her head back against his abdomen. "I know, it's just force of habit and the ability to do it in that instance. It's nothing against you my love and I'll try harder. I do know that I'm not alone and thank you for loving me."

"I've always loved you, so thank you for letting me." Shawn said while kissing the top of her head.

After the tickets were bought they all headed to bed. Tomorrow would be busy. They had to hand out invites to everyone they could and send a few to the people they couldn't walk to. They also wanted to go look at flowers and decide colors. They needed to order a cake and check out food options. They also wanted to talk to Catriona and make sure that she would perform the ceremony. The dress became clearer and the flowers were more in focus than any wedding dream she'd ever had before. Mellie had dreamt about her wedding since she was a little girl. Of course as she got older it didn't happen as often. Her lack of confidence had prevented her from finding love. Who knew all along it was right next to her?

When she woke up in the morning she could hear singing downstairs. She quickly jumped in the shower and threw on a flowy, white and green dress, brushed her teeth and her hair. Then decided to throw her hair in a messy bun because it had decided to frizz today. It didn't really help as there were pieces flying around her face and the base of her neck as soon as she got it pulled up. It was out of her face though so that was something. She walked downstairs to Shawn and Callum roaming around the kitchen attempting to make breakfast. They had started sausage and bacon and what Mellie assumed were going to be some kind of biscuits and gravy. She walked up to Callum and pecked him on the cheek then walked over to Shawn, who was at the stove and wrapped her arm around him. Callum walked over to her and handed her a cup of coffee.

"No thank you Dad. I'll have some of the sweet tea from the party. Thank you very much. I can't wait to taste whatever the two of you have been working on." Mellie said as she sat at the table. She didn't have to wait long until there were plates upon plates of food in front of her. They had really made a massive feast for what was to be a crazy busy day.

Callum and Shawn had made fried eggs, a pile of bacon and sausage, and giant biscuits and gravy. They ate more than their fill and then cleaned up after themselves.

"I know ya'll are having a busy day. I think i'm going to relax here, and maybe go on a hike around the property." Callum said. "I also need to take a nap already. A lot has happened in the past two days and these aging bones are tired."

"We're headed to town for the day. Wedding prep and planning. I'm waiting to start on the dress until Mom gets here. They should be here next Friday." Mellie said excitedly.

"I'm so happy that your mom will get to see me soon. Like me being me. Not the Wulver me."Callum said. Then he hummed his way up the stairs.

"Alright babe, I'm going to change and then we can head out. You look incredible by the way. Have I told you how much I love you lately?" Shawn asked walking his way to the stairs.

"Yep, but I'll always listen to it more." Mellie laughed. She quickly cleaned up from breakfast and grabbed her purse. She was ready to leave by the time Shawn came back down.

By the middle of the day they had chosen a color scheme of muted blues and greens. They had chosen a rustic theme in general and that included the cake. It was going to stand on wooden cake stands, with barely enough icing to cover the chocolate cakes so it looked almost like burch bark. There would be greenery and babys breath to decorate. They also decided on white cake cupcakes so there would be something everyone would like. They went to the seamstress shop and let her know that they would be back in a week with Mellie's mother and her dress to start the process. Then they were off to Catriona's house. They hadn't even reached the front door before Cat was standing there waiting with a smile on her face.

"Ah knew you'd be headed this wey th'day. Word spreads fleet in a such a small village. C'moan in a've git th' cuppa oan." Catriona said.

"Thank you Cat. That would be lovely." Mellie said.

They walked in and found their way to the couch. Catriona brought out the tea and scones right after they sat down. It was an exceptional earl grey tea and the scones were lemon blueberry and lemon poppyseed. They were quiet for a bit as they ate.

After they had finished their tea Catriona took everything back to the kitchen and returned with a couple sweets.

"Sae whit made ye come all the way over 'ere efter ye'v bin oot a'day?" Catriona asked.

"Well, as you know Shawn asked me to be his wife. We were going to wait until next summer when Dad and Grandpa could be here in human form, but now that it's not an issue we have decided to move the wedding up significantly. A month from this coming Saturday to be exact. We were wondering if you'd be willing to perform the ceremony? You've had such a profound impact in my life I couldn't imagine asking anyone else to do it."

Catriona started to cry. "Thir's nothing I'd lik' mair than tae be a pairt o' yer muckle day." They all stood up and she hugged Mellie and Shawn tightly. They stayed around and chatted for a while and then they headed out. Mellie and Shawn couldn't believe how long they'd been out. Pretty much all day. It was nearly dinner when they finally got back to the house. They made something quick and easy and hit the hay early that night. Not their normal, but it had been a long day and the guys were still dealing with jet lag.

CHAPTER THIRTY

The next week went by pretty quick. Filled with making things for the wedding, like place holders, decor, and small things that were easy enough to store. The guys built a beautiful archway that would be covered with flowers and chifon fabric. They even started to build benches that they would be using instead of chairs. It would be a great transition into the reception as everyone around them had offered their rectangular tables. Even the local businesses and churches were chipping in. The time before the rest of their families came flew by. Busy days at work with the Inn, and busy evenings at work with Catriona. Mellie had begun helping Cat organize her stacks and stacks of books. Angus and Callum had even talked about lining her walls with book shelves as to keep the historic documents off the floor. It was one thing after the other.

When the day their families would be there finally arrived it was like no time had passed at all. When Mellie finished up the lunch rush at the Inn she interviewed three very wonderful prospects. A man who had just arrived on the island would be working the kitchen. He had come from the mainland and loved what he had heard about Mellie and her family, and what they had done for the community. Basically, getting rid of the Brown's.

The other two interviews were two young girls from the local highschool. One was looking for weekend, and evening work. The other had just recently graduated and wanted to stick around for a couple years before college. She was looking for full time work, which would be great. That would mean Isla could have long term help whenever she needed it. Which to be honest since the divorce was all the time. When the intereviews were over Mellie headed home to shower and get the guys.

Mellie had it easy these days. One of the first things she did when she decided to live here full time was to get herself a boat. Nothing huge, but it got her to the mainland and back without having to wait on the ferry. It fit six other people and luggage, so size wasn't a problem. Mellie had a dock built right off the back of her property which was also a plus. They left the house right on time. Their families were getting a ride to the dock so they wouldn't have to go far. It would take them roughly six hours to get there and back. They'd be back at home right before Catriona would arrive with dinner. It was a well oiled machine, or at least that's what Mellie hoped it would be.

They had just hopped out of the boat when a car pulled up. Mellie was so excited she went running to the car. Practically tore the door off the hinges, but jumped back when she saw who was driving. Archie Brown himself He looked completely different. He sat with his head down and averted eye contact with Mellie, Angus and Callum. Their guests looked incredibly uncomfortable as well. Mellie can guess it had been the quietest ride in their entire lives.

"Thank you, Mr. Brown, for making sure our families arrived to the dock. What do I owe you?" Mellie asked completely professionally.

"Ye, ye owe me nothing Mellie. Twas mah pleasure." He said nervously.

"Nonsense. You're doing honest work and I will pay you. That's all I requested from the start. Do good work and treat people well, and we won't have any problems." Mellie said. She handed him 100 pounds.

" Ah cannae tak' that. Tis far tae much for something so small."

"Then consider the extra a tip." Mellie said as she and Callum loaded the bags onto the boat.

"Than' ye." He said. He got back in the car and drove away.

It was a pretty quiet trip back to the house. Six hours of beautiful sights and still water. When they got home Catriona and her sons were just pulling into the driveway. Mellie's mom and grandma ran straight up to Cat and helped unload the car after some brief hugs. They brought the food into the house and set it on the table. Angus and Callum carried in the bags and helped Shawn's dad in. Mellie set the table and with big hugs said goodbye to Catriona and her sons. When everything was ready, they all sat down and began to pass the serving plates.

"This looks incredible doesn't it Mom?" Mellie asked.

"It sure does! Your house is also amazing! I can't believe you set all this up so fast."

"It helped a lot that the entire town has been supporting us the whole time." Mellie responded.

"Ok ok ok… Enough of this talk. The wedding!" Amelia said.

"Calm down Grandma lol! Let's eat first"

"Absolutely not. Two weeks isn't nearly enough time to do all this. Must talk now" she said with her mouth full.

"Ok… We've got the benches made. Or at least most of them. All the neighbors and their businesses have offered the tables for the reception.

Cat and Isla are taking care of catering. We've ordered the cake. Dad and Callum made the archway. We just have to decorate it. Seriously Grandma. The only thing we still have to do is take care of the dress. We have an appointment to take care of that in the morning. We've already passed out and mailed all the invites. Isla is bringing her bartender and the liquor since no one will be there drinking that day. It's truly all taken care of."

"Speaking of the dress Mel. I brought it like you asked, but I also have another surprise. We brought Amelia's dress as well." Aileen said

"Are you serious?! I love your dress Grandma. I've only seen pictures but it's absolutely stunning." Mellie said happily.

"It was stunning dear. Now it's barely holding on by a thread. There are some salvageable parts and I'd love to see a piece or two in your dress." Amelia said with love in her eyes.

"Of course! I can't wait to see what we can make together!" By the time they had finished eating it was beyond time for bed. As they were going to their rooms Mellie heard a scream followed by a girlish laugh. Mellie ran into her grandparents room only to see her grandpa chasing Amelia all around the room as a squirrel. As Mellie stepped in her grandpa ran up Amelia's leg. Shawn walked in and saw what was happening. Callum and Aileen walked in the room to see Amelia on the floor rolling around and laughing. Mellie was doubled over laughing with Shawn. Callum started to chase his dad around. Aileen was crying.

"What's wrong sweety?" Callum asked.

"Oh, nothing. This is just wonderful. The freedom the two of you have now is crazy. It's a beautiful thing to see." Aileen said.

Without further hesitation Callum changed into a cat and started running after his dad. By the time it was over everyone in human form was rolling around the floor laughing. When Callum nipped Angus, Angus changed into a dog and the whole thing started again. It was a playful ten minutes, before Mellie could sense them getting tired.

"Alright boys! Let's call it quits for the night so you have energy to function tomorrow!" She laughed.

With that, they all said their goodnights, and drifted deeply into a well deserved and restful sleep. When Mellie's alarm went off the next morning the whole house was already alive with delicious smells and laughter.

Mellie got dressed and threw her hair in a low ponytail, brushed her teeth and washed her face. When she hit the kitchen the table was overwhelming. There were biscuits and four different types of jam. Coffee, hot tea, iced tea, and water. Angus was making what looked like a million eggs and Callum was flipping a half ton of bacon. Mellie knew the ladies wouldn't have time to enjoy much because of their early appointment at the dress maker's shop but they grabbed coffee and iced tea and a basketful of biscuits and jelly. Then with a brief goodbye to their guys and grabbing the dresses they were off to the seamstress.

CHAPTER THIRTY-ONE

The town was barely awake when they got to the center. Isla's pub was hopping, but then again it always was. The seamstress saw them headed her way and unlocked the door.

"Guid mornin' lassies. C'moan in a've git th' cuppa oan." Claire said happily. She had been looking forward to this for weeks.

"We'd love some tea. We also have biscuits and jam with us. This is my mom, Aileen and my grandmother, Amelia." Mellie said.

"Sae happy tae catch up wi' ye two lassies. Ah see two bags 'ere. Ur thare two dresses?" Claire asked.

"Yes! I didn't know but when they got here yesterday my grandmother had also brought what remains of her dress. I have pictures so you can see how lovely it was. I want to use a couple pieces from both if we can." Mellie said hopefully.

"Ah dinnae mynd usin' pieces fae both dresses. A'm excited tae see thaim. An new take on an old tradition and im here for it." Claire said. She was an amazing seamstress despite her youth. She had just graduated high school and took over her grandmother's shop. It had been a slow increase in business but she had gotten there. It had taken roughly 3 months for the townspeople to love her the way that they had loved her grandmother.

Claire walked them back to her shop after double checking that she had locked the front door. She had blocked out this whole day for Mellie's dress and no one was getting in the way of that.

"Ok, Claire so here's what I was thinking. Form fitting, but still etherial. I want fantasy vibes, but still a snatched waste. I would love cap sleeves or even long sleeves if we have the right fabric. I would also love a small train. Nothing that will need tending to, but something that will flow on the ground a bit. I would love lace accents. Possibly even lace sleeves of some sort. Please no stiff lace. I would like it to be just as flowy as the rest. Does any of that make sense?" Mellie let it all out. Claire had taken notes and immediately started drawing the basic outline.

"Ah think we can do most o' that. Can ah see th' dresses that ye two brought in? A'd loue tae git an idea o' th' fabric we hae tae wirk wi'." Claire asked Amelia and Aileen.

Aileen opened her bag first. The dress was hideous. Mostly made of stiff fabrics, and tulles with a sheen. The dress had yellowed over time and had some worn areas due to incorrect storage. It had an obnoxious high neck and poofy shoulders. It had an enormous bow on the back and a cathedral train. The only redeeming qualities it had were the pearl strands. They were completely intact and in wonderful condition. They were real pearls from her grandmother's wedding day. After careful consideration Mellie decided to use those on the back. She wanted a low back and decided to accent the back of the dress with pearls.

When Amelia opened her bag their eyes flew open. The dress was a mess to put it mildly, but not because it was ugly. It was a mess because of the age of the dress. The majority of the material was deteriorating to nothing. It was your typical 50's style wedding dress. Tea length and made of natural fabrics. This had caused some discoloration. It had a train which must have been an add on, Claire thought. It wasn't done often back then. The fabric was soft and flowy lace. Claire knew right away that it would be the sleeves that Mellie had mentioned. It was held together enough that it could do with some bleaching.

"'Ere ur mah thoughts we use th' pearls from yer moms dress. Drape thaim o'er yer back. I will just have to restring thaim. That wull tak' no time. I ken ye didn't know there was a train on your grandma's dress. We kin uise that fur sleeves. Ah wull tak' a little piece tae mak' sure ah kin bleach it. If ah cannae ah think ah kin dye it a sage green tae gang wi' th' color scheme." Claire said as she continued to draw her ideas.

They spent the entire day there and by the time they left the dress was well on it's way to completion. Mom and Grandma had a bit of an emotional moment when they say the pieces of their dresses placed on to Mellie's. By the time they got back to the house it was dinner time. When they walked onto the property their jaws dropped. It looked like all the benches were done and the arch was complete. People had started to drop off the tables. Everything looked like it was well on the way to completion. The guys were inside doing what the ladies assumed was dinner. Spaghetti was the only thing they could cook with any success outside of breakfast.

It was as they suspected a very meat heavy spaghetti. Delicious as they knew it would be. But oh, so heavy. When they were full to the brim it wasn't over yet. Callum brought out a strawberry shortcake that looked like he had worked on it for hours.

"Babe, are these strawberries the wild ones along the forest?" Mellie asked impressed.

"Yes my love. I decided after such a long day for all of us that we deserved a nice treat. I hope ya'll have room for it." He chuckled.

"We'll make room. This is too good to pass up." Angus said grabbing bowls and spoons.

"I even made whipped cream!" He said with a childlike excitement.

When they all had their fill of everything they cleaned up the kitchen and went on to bed. They knew the next week and a half would be hectic, but when Mellie laid down she slowly began to run her hand up Shawn's chest. He moaned and kissed her neck gently.

"My love," he groaned, "there is nothing I'd like more than to make sweet love to you. However, I am so tired. If I promise to wake up up with a sweet surprise can we rest tonight?"

"Of course my sweet man. I am beyond exhausted as well and could use a long night's sleep." Mellie said laying her head on his chest. It took no time at all before they were fast asleep wrapped around each other as always.

Mellie awoke the next day with a hand gently finding its way down her torso. Shawn slowly ran his index finger along the waist band of her panties. She shivered and moaned a tired moan. When he slid his hand below the wasteband she inhaled sharply, rolled towards him and kissed him passionately on the lips. His hand found its way lower until it cupped her heat. She worked herself against his palm to cause friction. His index and middle finger found their way into her folds.

"Oh, love you're so wet for me." Shawn whispered into her ear. It sent goosebumps through her whole body. He lifted his left hand to her breast and pinched her nipple. She then found her way to his ever growing erection and freed him from his boxer briefs. She began to work her hand up and down his cock. She removed her hand so she could quickly slide her panties down her legs. She kicked them off and with no notice was straddling him. He moaned deeply as she slowly slid onto him. She slowly moved her hips in circles while she moved up and down.

They were making love so gently and intensely that even her orgasms, while all encompassing, were slow and gentle. They made love for what seemed like the equivalent of a heavenly eternity. He flipped them softly and began to slide in and out of her with such tender strokes she lost herself in it.

"I don't know how long I'm going to last." Shawn breathed out in between thrusts.

'Babe, don't hold on for me. I'm 100 percent satisfied." Mellie said through pleasure

Shawn continued his thrusts and picked up speed. He came and when she felt him release she came again.

They laid there for what seemed like an eternity. Just soaking each other in. Shawn was the type of person who Mellie knew would never not love every single thing about her. She felt desired and she hoped he felt the same way. They jumped in the shower and headed downstairs. Their week was going to be so busy but with the best ending probably in the history of endings.

The week went by incredibly quickly. Mellie and Shawn talked to Isla about the food. Isla now had enough help that it would be no issue without Mellie. They were making all the Scottish staples: haggis, Cullen Skink, Cranachan, venison and smoked salmon. They would also bring appetizers and fruit bowls. Not to mention all the alcohol one could drink. It was going to be an amazing party. They had arranged the benches and the arch way. The flowers would be arriving Saturday morning and the florist would be decorating with Catriona and her helpers. The cake would also arrive Saturday morning. When Friday rolled around Mellie took Aileen and Amelia back to the seamstress with her. She had received a call late Thursday night that the dress was ready, and needed to be fitted.

Claire was there at the door when they arrived with an excited look on her face.

"Good morning, Claire! How's your morning going?" Mellie asked while giving Claire a warm hug.

"Better now that ye'r 'ere. Ah cannae wait fur ye tae see th' dress! C'moan!" Claire said full of excitement.

Mellie walked into the back room and started to cry when she saw it.

It was everything she'd ever dreamed of. It was a feather light material and Mellie couldn't wait to try it on. She stepped into the dressing room followed by Claire. Claire stepped out of her clothes and Claire put a piece of plastic down so the dress wouldn't get dirty from the floor. Mellie stepped into the dress and as Claire slid it up her body, it felt like butter. Her arms went into the soft lace sleeves, and she started to cry. When Claire had buttoned up the back and clipped on the pearls it was time to show Aileen and Amelia. Mellie stepped out of the dressing room and tears started flowing from everyone's eyes. Amelia walked up and ran her hands gently over the sleeves. Aileen walked around the back and just admired the pearl work. They couldn't believe all the work that had gone into the dress in less than a week.

"Oh my goodness Claire! It's the most beautiful dress I've ever seen." Amelia said.

"It looks like you were born to wear this dress. Not to mention the small little nods to our dresses. You did an amazing job." Aileen said with tears streaming down her face.

"Twas mah honor! Ah loved every second o' making this dress. Ah cannae wait tae see Shawn's reaction. This weekend is aff tae be incredible." Claire said.

"Claire, it is bound to be the best day of my life. I can't wait to see you there." Mellie went in back with Claire and changed. Claire placed her gown into a black bag and handed it to her. She handed Claire a check for the remaining balance of the dress and some extra. When Claire looked at the check her eyes started to water.

"Whin ah took the business over efter grandma passed ah wasn't

sure th' folk in this toun win like me. Ye hae changed all that 'n' fur it, ah ta. Ah will see ye th'morra fur the special day." Claire said as she walked Mellie back to the front of the shop.

Mellie took the dress as she, Amelia and Aileen walked into the warm afternoon. They needed to get home and make sure everything was going well with the guys. When they walked up the drive the house looked like a different place. There were big tents up with tables everywhere. Another big tent where a dance floor was being built. Soft fabrics were being draped over everything. They were olive green and dusty pink in color and lovely.

Shawn was around back by the grill. Mellie ran into the house and snuck the dress into the closet in her mom's room and then walked outside.

"How did the dress fitting go?" Shawn asked while flipping a burger.

"It was amazing! I can't wait for you to see me tomorrow." Mellie said while leaning in the give him a peck on the cheek. "How are things coming along here?"

"As you can see everything is right on schedule so far. Catriona's guys are here and that's going incredibly well. Everything should be ready for tomorrow." Shawn said as he removed the burgers from the grill. "I have pasta salad and fruit salad in the house for dinner. Let me call the guys in and we can eat. Then I'll send them home so we can get some much needed rest my love."

"That sounds perfect to me. Let me go in and set the table. Looks like we need four extra seats. Right?" Mellie asked.

"Yep, that's right. The buzz around this place has been incredible all day. I can't wait to make you mine officially." Shawn said as he wrapped an arm around Mellie. She grabbed the burgers and headed inside.

Amelia and Aileen had already set the table for the six of them. All the food and condiments were already out as well.

"Well, there sure isn't much for me to do is there?" Mellie asked.

"Nope. You sit down and relax." Aileen said lovingly.

"Will do. We will need four more chairs though. Cat's guys are here, and I want to feed them." Mellie said.

It took no time to add the table extension and the chairs. The guys all walked in together and washed their hands. When everyone was at the table the guys dug right in. The women waited a moment until the speedsters had stopped so they could get their plates. They chatted and ate. They must have sat around for a couple hours because by the time they were done it was pitch black outside.

"Thank you for dinner. We're headed hame. Yi'll need yer rest fur th' big day. Catriona wull be 'ere earlie tae let all the people git stairted. I was told to tell you, no working tomorrow. Juist soak in th' day." Said Catriona's grandson Braden.

"We are more than ok with that. We appreciate everything you've done to help and will do tomorrow. We'll see you tomorrow." Mellie said as she walked them to the door.

When they were gone Mellie let out a big sigh.

"What's wrong love?" Shawn asked.

"Absolutely nothing. I've just beyond grateful for the warm welcome this town has given us, and for all the help and work that's going in to the wedding. I am also extremely tired, and think I need to head to bed." Mellie said yawning widely.

With that Mellie headed off to bed and was pretty sure that she was asleep before her head hit the pillow.

Chapter Thirty-Two

When Mellie rolled over hours later to turn off her alarm clock she was already smiling. It was the day she'd dreamed about since she was a child and knew that it would surpass any dreams she'd ever had. Shawn had slept in the spare room last night and promised that he'd be at Cat's already this morning so they wouldn't see each other. You know tradition and all. Mellie had just gotten out of the shower and wrapped herself in her robe when she heard a light knock at her bedroom door.

"Come in!" She yelled from the bathroom. Her mom walked in and gave her a big hug.

"Shawn's been gone for about an hour. The florist is here. Decorators have been here for hours and Isla is on her way with her people. The cake will be here in a couple hours. Hair and makeup are on their way as well. Isla says she will be up to get ready after she gives all the information she feels will be helpful. Looks like everything's working exactly as it should." Aileen said.

"Mom, that was a lot of information before my coffee, but I think I got it." She joked.

"Grandma's bringing up breakfast in just a bit. Your only job today is to relax and get ready. We've got this for you." Aileen said.

"Thanks Mom. Don't forget you two have to get ready as well." Mellie said.

"I'm sure you won't let us forget it either." Aileen said.

"Of course I won't. This is your day too." She laughed. It was about twenty minutes later when Amelia walked in with bacon, eggs, and toast. There was a bowl of the remaining fruit salad from last night on the tray as well.

"Thank you so much Grandma. This looks wonderful." Mellie said giving her a hug.

"Isla said she'll be up in a bit with mimosas. Did you teach her about those?" Amelia asked.

"Yes, I did. I added them to the breakfast and brunch menu right away when I was helping out. She loves them. She thinks they're good at all times of the day. I must agree." Mellie laughed.

The house and grounds didn't stay quiet for long. Hair and makeup were up along with the florist. She handed Aileen some boxes which they all guessed were the flowers. The photographer came in and started taking 'get ready with me' pictures. That was fun for everyone. The mimosas made their way up and were flowing freely. Light on the champagne so that they stayed away from inebriation . It wasn't long before hair tools and makeup brushes were figuratively flying everywhere. Time passed so fast that before they knew it the time had come.

Mellie passed on the first look pictures. She wanted to see his genuine reaction when she walked down the aisle. Amelia was being escorted to her front row seat along with Angus when Mellie headed down the stairs with Isla. Her mother and father were waiting at the bottom. Aileen did ok with the first look as she had just seen the dress the day before, but Mellie hadn't even hit the bottom of the stairs before he was a sobbing mess. He walked up to Mellie and wrapped her in his arms. When he pulled away he turned her around like they were dancing. When he saw the pearl details on the back his breath hitched. He recognized them right away from Aileen's dress. Then he saw the sleeves. He, just like everyone else had only seen pictures of his mothers dress but he knew that fabric.

"These sleeves. They were on my mom's dress right?" He questioned with tears welling in his eyes again.

"You recongnized them so quickly. We decided to use the fabric that she had made into her train for my sleeves." Mellie said wiping his tears away. "Be careful you're going to make me cry Dad."

"You look beautiful Mel. I'm so excited to see this day." Callum said. Mellie's mom handed her the bouquet and they walked towards the back door.

"I hope he thinks I'm beautiful." Mellie said nervously, mainly to herself.

"If he doesn't think you're beautiful he's either blind or crazy." Aileen said laughing.

With that they opened the door. When the door opened Highland Cathedral started playing for her processional. She slowly walked down the island with her mom and dad on either side of her. When they turned a small corner at the bottom of the stairs she got her first glimpse of Shawn.

When he saw her he covered his face with his hands and bent at the waste. When he stood back up he turned to his father.

"I can't believe she's mine Dad. She's the most beautiful woman I've ever seen and now she's going to be my wife." Shawn said to his dad.

"You are certainly one lucky man, Son." he said.

As Mellie walked down the aisle all eyes scanned from Shawn to her over and over again. People were teary eyed, snapping pictures and taking videos. When she got to to the archway her mom and dad gave her a hug. Catriona didn't ask who was giving her away as a woman is a human and not something to be given. She stepped up and faced Shawn.

"A thousand welcomes tae ye wi' yer marriage. May ye be healthy all yer days. May ye be blessed wi' lang life 'n' peace. May ye graw wi' goodness. 'N' wi' riches." Catriona started off. "Ah know you've written your own vows. Noo it th' time tae say thaim. As ye say yer vows exchange rings please mah dears."

"I have dreamed of this day since we were children Mellie." Shawn said. "I can't remember a time in my life when I didn't want, no need, you in it. We have grown up together, playing together, fought together and now we get to live and love together. I know our journey hasn't been easy and I know that we will have challenges, but I can't imagine anyone I'd rather experience them with. I can't wait to grow old with you." And he placed the ring on her finger. Mellie wiped the tears away from her eyes and held his hand tight for a moment before she started her vows.

"We have been friends since we were children, and I never thought it would grow into this love. We had so many firsts together. Our horses, school, fights, losing animals and so many others. I had my first shift with you, and I was scared. You were there to comfort me. When I was taken you saved me and when I hurt, you help me. I don't know what I did to deserve this love, but I'm so happy I have it, and I will work every day to show you how much I love you. I can't wait to start our lives together and see where life takes us next." She placed a wooden ring on his finger.

"Groom 'n' bride hae chosen tae conclude thair day wi' a traditional handfasting. This is a symbolic binding o' th' hands that inspired th' ters "bonds o'holy matrimony" 'n' tae "tie th' knot" through out history in mony different places 'n' in mony different ways 'n' in mony different bits o' th' world. Th' hauns o' th' bride 'n' groom wur bound as a sign o' thair commitment tae yin another. In mony places, rings were only available to the rich. While love knows no bounds. Th' cords ur nae permanent bit perishable as a reminder that a' hings o' th' material eventually return tae th' earth. Unlike th' bond 'n' th' connection that is loue whilk is eternal. Please join yer richt hauns." Catriona started the handfasting with an explanation.

As they joined hands, Catriona wrapped the cords around their wrists in a figure eight infinity symbol.

"Bride 'n' groom this cord is a symbol o' th' lives ye hae chosen tae live th'gither. Up 'til this moment, ye hae bin separate in thought, word 'n' action. As yer hauns ur bound th'gither by this cord, sae tae, shall yer bides be bound as yin. Kin ye forever be yin, sharing in a' hings, in loue 'n' loyalty fur a' time tae come.

With yer hauns 'n' hears noo bound, ah wid lik' tae share wi' ye a traditional Irish blessing.

May th' road rise tae catch up wi' you.
May th' win' be aye at yer back.
May th' sun shine taps aff upon yer face, the rains fall soft
upon th' fields.
May th' light o' friendship guide yer paths together.

May th' laughter o' bairns grace th' halls o' yer home.
May th' joy o' living fur yin another trip a smile fae yer lips,
a twinkle fae yer eye.
*   And whin eternity beckons, at th' end o' a lee heaped heich*
wi' loue kin th' guid laird embrace ye wi' th' arms that hae
nurtured ye th' hail length o' yer joy-filled days.
'N' th' day, kin th' spirit o' loue fin' a dwelling steid in yer
hears.
Amen

Noo ye kin winch yer bidie in."

And with that Mellie and Shawn let their lips join. Everyone stood, clapped, and yelled for close to an eternity. Isla and Shawn's dad walked down the aisle and stood under the dance floor tent. Shawn and Mellie quickly followed to hug and shake hands with their guests. When they had seen everyone, cocktail hour started so that pictures could be taken. They decided to take pictures on the dock and in the woods. What better than the places they felt most at home. Mellie walked the photographer back to the tree they knocked down on their first night in the house together. Mellie lay on the tree and Shawn climbed right over her. He was between her legs lifted up by his arms. He leaned down and kissed her gently while the photographer took a couple pictures of them on the tree. She had no idea why this tree was special, but these pictures were going to be amazing.

When pictures were done being taken they made their way back to the food tents. Everyone was either eating or in line to get their food. The night was a blur, but it was so much fun. A night they surely would never forget. Mellie was ready to begin her life with her husband in this new town. She knew it wouldn't be easy and she knew that people would probably come for her and her town at some point but she didn't care in this moment. She was going to enjoy this life as long as she possibly could.

ACKNOWLEDGEMENTS

It's impossible to thank just one person.

Thank you Amanda for pushing me to do this! I've come to love it more than I ever thought possible. Even more thanks because you are my publisher/employer, and most importantly my friend. I couldn't have even began this journey without you giving me the confidence needed to know that I could.

Thank you to the Coven and The Silly Goose Society! I don't know what I would do without you guys! Thank you for believing in me. Especially when I didn't believe in myself.

To Susan: thank you for your editing genius! Thank you for also reassuring me multiple times that I had a good story(especially upping my confidence in the spicy scenes).

To Amy, Martha, Ashleigh, and everyone else this journey has placed in my path. I truly love you all!

Finally to my family: to my kiddos, Israel, mom, and sister. This has been a hard year with a lot of loss. Thank you for loving me through the worst of it and I love you all to the moon and back.